The
Fledgling

The
Fledgling

ELIZABETH CADELL

William Morrow & Company, Inc.
New York 1975

1   2   3   4   5   79   78   77   76   75

Library of Congress Cataloging in Publication Data

Cadell, Elizabeth.
  The fledgling.

  A novel.
  I. Title.
PZ3.C11427Fl 3 [PR9499.3.C3]   823'.9'12   74-17473
ISBN 0-688-02880-2

The
Fledgling

Chapter One

The room was large, richly furnished and extremely cold. From a cavernous fireplace surmounted by marble cherubs, a small pile of logs sent out picturesque wreaths of smoke but no perceptible warmth. Close by were two high-backed, brocade-covered chairs, and in these two elderly Portuguese ladies sat drinking their morning coffee. Tall, dragon-embroidered Chinese screens behind them protected them from drafts. On a low table beside one of the chairs was an embroidery frame; beside the other stood a long-legged, lacquered workbox. Between the chairs, on a silver-topped table, was a coffeepot flanked by delicate china cups and a selection of sweet biscuits. A maid was in attendance.

The ladies, sisters named Pilar and Piedade, could at no time have been called merry; their thin, proud-nosed countenances were seldom lit by laughter. On the other hand, they did not often appear out of spirits. Their normal expression was one of placid dignity, which might have been attributed to the ease and elegance of their lives, but which in fact had a deeper source: their inherited talent for ignoring problems. Trivial ones they left to be dealt with by their servants. Weightier ones, such as mounting debts and shrinking assets, they consigned to the care of God. On these twin stabilizers, staff and Saviour, the domestic ship sailed smoothly. So when the sisters were seen, as they were to be seen this morning, sunk in gloom, it could be assumed that a crisis of unusual proportions had occurred.

Not only in this room but throughout the great house, the heavy atmosphere prevailed. Only the mother of Pilar and Piedade—the ancient, widowed Jesuina, now withdrawn into a half-world of her own—remained unaware of the depression that hung over the household. Everyone else, from Pilar and Piedade through descending ranks of retainers to the kitchen and laundry staffs in the basement, had spent the morning wiping away tears and lamenting. Their child, the child born in this house ten years before, the motherless infant they had all loved and reared and cherished, was to leave them. She was to go away. She was to leave Lisbon, leave Portugal, the land of her birth. This afternoon, her father would drive her to Santa Appolonia station, and the Sud Express would bear her northward on the first stage of her journey to the land of mist and snow and heretics: England.

The child was the great-niece of Pilar and Piedade, but they had long regarded her as a daughter. Was she not named Vitorina Piedade Jesuina Azevedo, binding her to her mother's family? But her father was, unfortunately, English, and her surname was Brooke, and she was known not as Vitorina or Piedade or Jesuina but by her father's name for her: Tory. And her father, Edmund Brooke, had decreed that she was to go to school in England. He had chosen a Protestant school, and though he seldom asserted his authority, Pilar and Piedade knew that it was useless to challenge it.

The decision to take his daughter away from the local convent, which she had attended as a day pupil since the age of five, had been taken some months earlier, but throughout the subsequent negotiations the household had been sustained by the comfortable certainty that something would happen to prevent the plan from being put into operation. Some hitch would surely occur. The school in England might be full, Tory might show herself unwilling to be sent away, Father Diogo might talk Edmund into changing his mind. But the school had a place for Tory; Tory had uttered no protest or objection—and Father Diogo had talked to no purpose. And time had marched inexorably onward, bringing at last this day on which she was to leave.

The knowledge that she would return to Lisbon for the Easter holidays in three months' time brought no comfort to her great-aunts. How could anything ever be the same again? The child would have adopted new ways, would have imbibed new and dangerous beliefs; she was as good as lost to them.

Pilar, the elder of the two sisters, handed her cup to the maid and made a gesture of dismissal. As the door closed, she addressed Piedade.

"Why did we refuse to believe that this could happen? Why should we have hoped that her father would allow her to continue at the convent? Don't you remember what happened three years ago?"

"Two," corrected Piedade. "Of course I remember; how could anyone forget? He ordered his car and told Mademoiselle Barrault to get Tory ready, and then he drove off to the Protestant church of . . . what is its name?"

"Saint George. Saint George is the patron saint of England. It was a Sunday."

"Naturally it was a Sunday. Protestants do not pray during the week. He came back from this church and said that in future Tory would be Catholic one week and Protestant the next. Even Father Diogo could not make him see reason, that a child could not be Catholic and Protestant at once, especially as she was baptized a Catholic, here in the chapel of this very house, and by Father Diogo himself."

"That is what I meant. If he could do a thing like that, we should have known that he would make trouble about schools. We don't even know that they will take her to Mass every second and fourth Sunday."

"Have you seen those ugly clothes the poor child has got to wear?"

"It is a uniform. At school, she will have to look like everybody else."

"Does a uniform help a child to learn better? A gray skirt, a blouse such as a peasant would wear, shoes far too heavy for her poor little feet. Everything ugly, ugly, ugly."

"We will tell Mademoiselle Barrault to see that she is properly dressed during the holidays."

"I have been thinking about Mademoiselle Barrault. Do you suppose she will now wish to retire?"

"No."

"She has never told her age, but she is older than I am, older even than you. She must be seventy. If Tory is no longer to be under her care, then—"

"There are many other things she can do. Nobody is so good at matching my wools and your silks, nobody can get things as cheaply as she can, nobody in the shops has ever succeeded in selling her anything that was not exactly what she wanted. I find that kind of shopping more and more fatiguing; she can make herself very useful."

"But as she is paid by Edmund, perhaps he will wish to send her back to France. With an adequate pension, of course."

"If that is what he wishes, he will say so. But there is no need for us to put the idea into his head."

"What put it into his head to choose England? Why not Switzerland? Why not a good convent in France, where those nice little grandchildren of the Comtesse were sent? Why England?"

"It is, after all, his own country."

"Has he ever spoken of it? Has he ever been there, set foot there since his wife died? No. And then to announce that he has chosen an English school, a Protestant school, and Tory was to begin there in the January term . . . this is what I object to. If this had happened when our mother was still in her right mind, it would have killed her."

"True. But, thank God, she can understand nothing. For myself, I am not going to say that sending Tory away to school was not in some ways wise; she has outstripped her classmates here, and as she grows older she will need more companionship out of school hours. We, after all, are old. Mademoiselle Barrault is even older. But I agree with you that it need not, should not have been a Protestant school."

"And in England!"

They fell silent, recalling their last visit there. They had once been in the habit of paying occasional visits to English friends, taking their maids with them. But the last visit had indeed been the last. Gone were their friends' servants, gone the comforts that had enabled visitors to withstand the rigours of the climate. Gone were the crackling fires in their bedrooms, gone the English breakfasts taken at a table before their sitting-room fire. They were offered no midmorning coffee in front of the library fire. They could no longer enjoy English teas beside the drawing-room fire, with wafer-thin brown bread and butter, miniature sandwiches of cress or cucumber, delicious little scones and cakes. Gone were the dinners cooked by a first-class chef. Gone was the chef, and with him every vestige of elegance or ceremony, leaving only a drab life of labour in the kitchen. Pilar and Piedade, noting the lamentable changes, had done their best to help by suggesting that their own maids dust the furniture or polish the silver—but the silver had been put away and the dust left where it was, and they had been made to understand, in the politest way possible, that the only manner in which they could help was by removing themselves and their maids as soon as possible. It was to this country, to these conditions, they now pointed out to one another, that Tory was to be sent.

"It is no use objecting." Pilar spoke out of a long silence. "Edmund is the child's father."

Silence fell again while they recalled that, as well as being the child's father, he was the man who was paying not only for the apartments he and Tory had occupied in the house since the death of his wife but also for a large proportion of the household expenses. He had accepted without protest the transfer of the wages of several servants from their payroll to his. He had been generous, this they admitted, but after all, as Pilar pointed out more than once, he was getting richer all the time, while they were growing poorer.

The process of impoverishment had been a rapid one. For generations past, careless hands had been scattering riches from a fund so deep that it had been regarded as inexhaustible. Only when Jesuina, widow of the last male of the Lisbon branch of the family, dipped her hands into the crock to find marriage portions for her three daughters, Pilar, Piedade and Margarida, was it found to be empty.

The discovery caused shock but no panic. Jesuina reasoned that the gradual, discreet sale of the contents of the house would supply all that was needed for her own lifetime; the girls would of course marry rich husbands. Nobody need know that the tapestries and pictures and ornaments of the celebrated Casa Fenix were going steadily to the salesrooms.

The house, standing at the junction of two of the highest streets of Lisbon, rose—as its name of phoenix implies—from the ruins of a mansion destroyed in the great earthquake of 1755. Its exterior was an indigestible blend of Moorish, Manueline and Joanine; its interior resembled a miniature cathedral, with high arches, vaulted ceilings, elaborately carved galleries, aislelike corridors, marble floors and a profusion of winged cherubs. The chapel, panelled in beautiful Brazilian wood, glowed with gold and gems. Golden statuettes of saints stood in niches round the wall, jewels winked from the altar cloth and from the blue robes of the Virgin.

The overall effect was sumptuous, for at the time the house was built, the owners had been at the receiving end of a flow of gold and diamonds from their newly-discovered mines in Brazil. For two hundred years they had lived like princes—benevolent princes, for the family tradition was one of openhandedness, especially to the Church. In every room were treasures. The contents of the chapel were regarded as sacrosanct, but when the time of scarcity came there were countless assets throughout the rest of the house for Jesuina to fall back on. Falling back on them, she and her daughters continued their serene, elegant, expensive existence, closing up successive rooms as they denuded them of their contents.

Perhaps rumours of ruin spread; at all events, few suitors made their appearance to ask for the hand of Pilar or Piedade or Margarida. Those who, undeterred by rumours, presented themselves were dismissed as being not quite up to standard. This was later seen to have been not only high-handed but improvident, for the three daughters remained unwed. Only the youngest, Margarida, at length found a husband—a prosperous merchant from the Portuguese possession of Macau, who carried her overseas, leaving her mother and sisters to a life divided between selling and spending.

Four years before, at the age of eighty-six, Jesuina had decided to move downstairs to the half-empty, echoing rooms on the ground floor once known as the state apartments. These adjoined the chapel, in which she now spent most of her time, seated on her velvet-covered, thronelike chair before the altar. Pilar and Piedade moved into the rooms she had vacated. They were then in their early sixties, still slim and upright, still imposing, still elegant. They passed their lives between social occasions, prayer and directing the welfare of their great-niece, Tory, granddaughter of their sister Margarida.

Margarida had died in Macau. Edmund Brooke, an industrialist with headquarters in Lisbon, had during a business trip to Macau met, fallen headlong in love with and married Margarida's only child, the seventeen-year-old Vitorina. The couple had settled at the Casa Fenix to await the coming of their first child and to look round for a suitable home for themselves. The baby—another Vitorina—was born, and was left with her great-aunts while Edmund took his beautiful young wife to England, to show her off to his relations.

Two months later, he was back at the Casa Fenix—a widower, dazed with grief. The plans for an establishment of his own were abandoned, and he agreed to Pilar and Piedade's proposal that he should rent a suite of rooms in the house. As his business trips were frequent and worldwide, he was seldom at home, and it fell to Pilar and Piedade to supervise the upbringing of his daughter. They appointed first a nurse and later a companion for the child, the companion being an elderly Frenchwoman named Mademoiselle Barrault, who had once instructed them in French and music. Transferred to Edmund's staff, she trained the small Tory in manners and deportment, drew up her menus, accompanied her on outings and implanted in her something of her own wary, self-protecting attitude towards life.

Mademoiselle Barrault was facing the departure of her charge with mixed feelings. She was aware that the small measure of authority she had exercised over Tory had long since ended; she was dealing with a mind as active, as adult as her own, and she knew that her orders were obeyed and her advice taken only when they fitted in with Tory's own plans. But she was secure and comfortable, she was virtually the mistress of Edmund Brooke's staff, her duties were light and her salary generous. Dreading a possible curtailment of these privileges, she had hoped even more fervently than Pilar or Piedade that something would occur to make Tory's father change his mind.

Something had indeed occurred, but it was a difficulty that had been overcome. Tory was to have travelled to England by train in the company of two English girls, twins named Paget, and their mother. Their father had set off by car, taking with him the heavy luggage—Tory's as well as the twins'—and tickets had been bought and reservations made not only on the Sud Express to Hendaye but also on the train from Hendaye to Paris and on the night ferry across the English Channel. Their passports were in order; everything was in readiness for their departure. At this point it was discovered that the twins had come out in spots. The doctor was summoned and made his pronouncement: chicken pox. To travel was out of the question.

The news created a difficult situation at the Casa Fenix. The problem was to find in so short a time a substitute, someone reliable in whose care Tory could travel—for she had never gone anywhere unaccompanied. Who, Pilar asked Piedade, could go with her to England? Certainly not themselves; they would not be able to make their arrangements in so short a time. Not Mademoiselle Barrault; she was too old. So who?

They did not consider the possibility of Edmund's accompanying his daughter. It had long been accepted that England, for him, was a place of torturing memories. He went on business trips to most other parts of the world but invariably left the English side of his affairs to his colleagues. Not once had he spoken of his dead wife, not once had anyone in the house ventured to mention her name in his presence. So Edmund would certainly not go. Then who?

It was through Edmund that an escort was found: an Englishman named Darlan, with whom for some years he had had a slight acquaintance. Mr. Darlan was a keen golfer and spent the winters in Estoril; Edmund had frequently played golf with him and had once or twice invited him to the Casa Fenix for a drink. Mr. Darlan now telephoned from the Estoril Club to say that he had just come in from playing a foursome, and understood from remarks heard during the game that there was difficulty about Edmund's daughter travelling to England by herself. By a fortunate chance, he himself happened to be travelling on the Sud Express on the same day; he would be only too happy to keep a fatherly eye on the child. He was to meet his sister at the Gare du Nord in Paris; he and she together would see Tory safely into the care of whoever was to meet her in London.

Pilar and Piedade, informed by Edmund of this offer, were much relieved, and invited Mr. Darlan to dine, and were reassured to find that he looked reliable and behaved with propriety. He was portly of figure, plain of face and bluff in manner. By the meal's end, he had made himself so agreeable that they agreed to his request to be shown over the house—a privilege rarely accorded now that so many rooms were closed.

Tory, sent down before dinner to be presented to him, disliked him on sight, and resented being spoken to as though she were six instead of ten. But she had long ago perfected the art of concealing her feelings, and she reminded herself that if he had not offered to

15

travel with her she might have been sent by air in the care of a TAP hostess, thus missing the novel experience of two nights in a train. After the exchange of a few polite sentences, she was permitted to retire, and Mr. Darlan, having no powers of divination, filed her as a mousy, well-mannered little thing, not pretty and certainly no conversationalist; one of those tongue-tied children out of whom monosyllables had to be dragged. But he had his own reasons for offering himself as escort on the journey, and it would not have suited him to be saddled with a chatty miss whose tongue wagged nonstop.

At noon on the day of departure, Tory went on a farewell tour of the house. She began in the basement, in which her special friends worked: Elisa, the laundry maid, Maria-Rosa, the cook, and the cook's assistants, Elena and Laurinda. The time Tory spent with them, the knowledge she picked up from listening to them, would have astounded her father and stunned her great-aunts. Though she was still very young, every servant in the house knew her discretion to be absolute; their secrets were as safe with her as hers were locked within herself.

From the basement, she went up to the warren of servants' rooms at the top of the house. Everyone there had a present for her, small but offered in love. She dried the tears of her donors, sent the presents to her room and changed into her travelling clothes. Then she went to the apartments of Pilar and Piedade.

Perhaps it was the knowledge that she was leaving that brought the scene into sharper focus than usual. She took in the picture and it sank into the recesses of her memory, to be retrieved in all its detail whenever she thought of her aunts. The spacious room, the brilliant dragons embroidered on the screens, the crucifix on the wall between two windows, the rugs spread beneath her aunts' feet to insulate them from the cold marble floor; her aunts, beautifully dressed as always, Pilar with snow-white hair piled high, Piedade with a gray plait encircling her head; their bracelets and brooches, their long, blue-veined hands.

Pilar spoke—in Portuguese; only with her father did Tory speak English.

"Are you feeling sad, my darling?"

"Not yet, Aunt Pilar. Perhaps when I get on the train . . ."

Pilar sighed.

"You look so much like your angel of a mother, but you do not act like her. She would have been so excited, so nervous, so unwilling to go from her home. You are calm, always calm, never showing your feelings. In that, you are like your father. You must try to be more like your mother. And you must never forget that you are a good Catholic, whatever your father may say."

"Father Diogo," Piedade said, "is going to write to a priest he knows in England, to ask him if he will tell the school to send you regularly to Mass. Don't forget always, every day, to say your Rosary. The one I gave you was blessed by Father Arnaldo; you must never lose it."

"Write and tell us everything, everything," Pilar begged. "If you do not like this school, you must tell us, and we shall insist that your father remove you at once." Her tears began to flow. "It is a great mistake for you to be sent away. Why should you be English all of a sudden? What shall we do without you?"

Tory had no suggestions. She sat motionless but relaxed, her expression serious and attentive, her mind elsewhere, lending, as always, a dutiful eye and a deaf ear. She never fidgeted, never interrupted; she had never been heard to contradict. She agreed with everything that was planned for her, and made her own arrangements later, for she had discovered that the easiest way through life was to set out obediently upon the appointed path and then slip away down a side turning. She had also discovered the usefulness of always speaking the truth; she had taken truth and polished it and made it into a weapon. If you told the truth, she had proved to herself, nobody could ever trip you up. It didn't have to be the whole truth; just as much as was necessary to meet the situation. Telling lies—she had observed this often among the servants or some of the girls at the convent—landed you into tangles that could never be straightened out.

"You will not have seen Mademoiselle Barrault this morning," said Piedade. "She sent a message to say that she had had a very bad night, worrying about your going so far away. You must remember to write many letters to her."

"Yes, Aunt Piedade."

"And now you must go and say good-bye to my mother. We shall all be in the hall to see you off when you leave. Go now, my child."

Tory went downstairs, lingering on every stair, as she had done all her life, to trace with a finger the names of early Portuguese kings intricately worked into the wrought-iron balustrade. At the curve of the great staircase, she saw below her the hall with its large black and white marble squares, polished and gleaming and—in her earlier years—frightening in its immensity. At hall level she found Angelina, once her own nurse and now transferred to the service of the aged Jesuina. Angelina addressed Tory in a worried tone.

"The Senhora is not in her rooms, Menina Tory. I waited here to tell you. She is very upset; she has gone back to the chapel to pray."

"Upset? But she doesn't know—"

"She knows nothing of your going away, no. It isn't that. She is upset, or she is pretending to be upset, who can say which? She says that Saint Christopher is not in his place."

"Oh. Is she hiding things again?"

"Yes. It is only a game—God knows it will be the last game that she will play—but it is a game that gives us maids a lot of trouble. She gets more and more clever at hiding things. Before, it used to be behind a chair, under a table—places easy to find. Now it is different. It took us two weeks to find the new slippers that—"

"But Saint Christopher?" Tory frowned. "She couldn't have taken him down from his place. She couldn't reach so high."

"By standing on one of the kneeling stools, she could reach up to the saint."

"But even so, think how heavy that statuette is."

"Heavy, yes, but no heavier, Menina Tory, than the marble bookrest she took from her room and hid in the chapel. It took us, Maria and Odette and myself, eight days to find it."

"When did she hide Saint Christopher?"

"It must have been just after early Mass this morning. She stayed in the chapel afterwards, as she always does, sitting in her place, saying her Rosary. Saint Christopher was still in his place. I left her for half an hour while I cleaned and tidied her bedroom. Maria and Odette swept the hall and the corridors and the other rooms. When I returned to the chapel to help the Senhora back to her room, she was sitting with tears on her cheeks, and she pointed to the empty niche and said that Saint Christopher had been stolen."

"*Stolen?*"

"That is what she always says when she hides things. Go to her, Menina. Perhaps she will not pretend with you. Perhaps she will tell you where she has hidden it. Not in her bedroom, certainly; I was there. Not in the other rooms, because Maria and Odette were there. So it must still be in the chapel."

"Did you look?"

"The three of us all looked. But it is strange that this time the Senhora did not help us to look. Other times, she has always helped us, pretending that she had no idea where the things could be. This morning, she only sat in her place in the chapel saying that it was no use wasting our time; the saint had been stolen."

"Did you ask her who stole it?"

"Odette asked her, and the Senhora acted very strangely. She closed her lips very tight, and put her finger on them and shook her head."

"Meaning that she wouldn't tell?"

"Yes. But it is impossible that anybody could have got in to steal anything. How could anyone get past Guilhermo at the courtyard gate? It would be impossible. Go and persuade the Senhora to come out, Menina, and we will go into the chapel and look more thoroughly."

Tory walked to the low, arched, studded door of the chapel. She pushed it open gently and went in, closing it behind her. Then she stood waiting for her eyes to become accustomed to the gloom.

19

The only light came from the small, circular window placed high on one of the walls. The door used by the priests who came to say Mass or to hear confessions was now closed.

It was this place, she knew, this dimly-lit shrine, this oval jewel box, that would live in her mind always. In all her future life, however long it might be, she would be able, simply by closing her eyes, to find herself back in this incense-saturated chamber lined with pale Brazilian wood, agleam with jewels, rich with the treasure brought long, long ago from Calicut and Cathay, from the gold and diamond mines of Brazil, from her mother's land of Macau. The crosses, the great Crucifix, the golden saints standing in their niches round the walls, the Virgin with her blue robe encrusted with gems, the tall, twisting gold candlesticks, the rows of high-backed, scarlet-and-gold chairs; here, where she was supposed to pray, she dreamed of far-off lands, of the long-buried noblemen and warriors who had founded the family, a family once great and powerful and now shrunk to three old women living among the relics of the past.

Her eyes went to the central chair in the front row. There sat Jesuina. Tory made her way to her, genuflecting as she passed the altar, and took one of the tiny, clawlike hands into her own. It was like holding an empty eggshell. The rheumy old eyes peered up at her without recognition. As long as she could remember, this was how Jesuina had looked—wrinkled, hunched, shuffling in gold-embroidered slippers, leaning on a rubber-tipped, gold-topped stick. Her long black gowns, her long ropes of pearls, her filigree brooches seemed changeless, like the sparse yellowish hair that was kept smooth at the back and had a high false fuzz in front. All that had changed through the years was the long, parchment-coloured face; the nose seemed to have grown thinner and longer, reaching down to a chin that curved upward to meet it.

"It's Tory, Aunt Jesuina." She had never addressed her as great-grandmother. "It's Tory. How are you?"

A gnarled finger of Jesuina's free hand came up and pointed, shaking, to the empty niche in which the statuette of St. Christopher had stood.

"Gone!" she croaked. "Gone! Look!"

Tory looked. Eight golden saints had always stood in niches round the walls, their names, in tiny gold letters, framed at the foot of each: Saints Christophe, João, Tiago, Bento, Pedro, António, Martinho and Sebastião. Long ago, in the days when the public had been admitted to the services, there had been wrought-iron grilles protecting the saints, but these had been removed when the Church of São Tiago had been built nearby and the chapel had reverted to the exclusive use of the family. Now the gate that gave entry from the courtyard was kept locked, and gatekeepers appointed to keep out intruders.

Tory, looking at the empty niche in which Saint Christopher had stood and should have been standing, could only wonder how the frail Jesuina had found strength enough to lift the statuette —only twelve inches high, but of solid gold—down from its place. She was not surprised that her great-grandmother had chosen Saint Christopher; it was Jesuina's favourite, an object of such exquisite workmanship that connoisseurs from many countries had sought permission to view it.

"The maids will find it again, Aunt Jesuina," she said reassuringly.

"No. It's gone. Taken away. Stolen. I saw."

"Whom did you see, Aunt Jesuina?"

"The thief. He didn't see me."

A thief—if there had been a thief—would have found it difficult to see the little figure in the high-backed chair. If he entered from the door that opened from the courtyard, he would find himself in semi-darkness and he might come and go without knowing that anybody but himself had been in the chapel. But thieves, Tory was certain, could not enter where there was a gatekeeper as alert as Guilhermo.

"Won't you come with me to your room, Aunt Jesuina?"

"Yes, yes. Help me up."

Tory put a hand under the bony elbow and steadied the wasted form. As she turned towards the door that led into the house, she felt Jesuina's hand tighten on her arm. She paused, certain that

Jesuina was about to say something; the mystery of the missing saint was about to be cleared up. But instead of speaking, Jesuina repeated the pantomime that Angelina had described: lips tight, a finger placed on them. She was going to keep her secret.

Tory led her to her room, kissed her gently on both cheeks and left her in the care of her maids. Going upstairs, she wondered whether she would ever see Jesuina again, and hoped that she would, for she loved her.

At the top of the stairs she saw the short, stout, tightly corseted figure of Mademoiselle Barrault awaiting her.

"Hurry, my child, hurry. You see, when I am not with you to attend to everything, you forget what you should do. Your father is waiting for you. Today, you are not to have your lunch with me; you are to have it with him in his study. He expects you to be ready, quite ready to leave for the station immediately after lunch. Come with me and I will show you your things."

Tory followed her to the rooms they occupied together. Her school beret, her school overcoat and gloves were on a chair. On the floor close by were a small suitcase and a straw basket of the open type, with two handles.

"Now please attend to me, my child." Mademoiselle Barrault, as always, spoke in French. "I have put some extra things into your suitcase. On the list the school sent, it said four vests, so I put in four of the kind you wear here, but I have also put in two long-sleeved woollen ones, which you can wear when it is very cold. They are ugly, but you must protect yourself against chills; the English climate is terrible, and it is also treacherous. I have packed extra blouses, and a dress and a shirt and of course your school uniform. In this little basket I have put books for you to read on the train, and some sandwiches and some fruit. You must not eat the apples before you wash them or peel them; this is very important. I have also put in a small towel and a little cake of soap, and some orange juice in case you are thirsty. You should put your gloves in the basket; you will need them when you get to Hendaye tomorrow morning. It will be very cold there; put on a warm vest. And don't lose any of your things; it isn't as if Mrs. Paget were with you, to remind you. Mr. Darlan will of course look after you, but he won't look after your luggage. Now kiss me and we will say a prayer to Our Lady. I shall not go downstairs to see you off; it would upset me too much. And now you must hurry to lunch with your father."

Making her way to the study, Tory rehearsed several topics of conversation. He would expect her to talk—everybody expected her to talk. Silence was said to be golden, but it also appeared to be anti-social. So she must talk—about what? Certainly not about the only thing she ever wanted to talk about with her father—namely, her mother and her mother's life in Macau. What did that leave? She had once studied the geography and the imports and exports of Argentina, ready to startle him on his return with a rain of interesting facts—but he had not returned from Argentina. His plans had been changed and it was Peru that she should have looked up. Where had he last been? On the golf course at Estoril. Did you have a good game? Were you in good form, bad form, this form, that form?

There had been a time, in her earlier childhood, when she had looked to her father for companionship. But just as she had reached the point at which she thought some contact might be established, he had vanished—to Japan, to New York, to Chile or Bangkok. One could not be forever beginning and progressing to no end.

He was standing by the window as she entered, and she went up to him and put up her cheek for his kiss. He put his hands on her shoulders and studied her.

"Not in your school uniform?"

"No. Mademoiselle Barrault thought I shouldn't wear it to travel in."

"I see." He pressed the bell and led the way to the table. "Have you said all your good-byes?"

"Yes."

"Your aunts will miss you."

She waited until she was seated before replying.

"Not Aunt Jesuina. She won't . . . she won't realize."

"I suppose not. But old people are sometimes very good at sensing what's going on. Was she upset?"

"Yes, but not about me. She's hidden Saint Christopher and they're all looking for him."

"Saint Christopher from the chapel?"

"Yes."

"Isn't that a bit too high and too heavy for her to have got hold of?"

"Angelina says she could have stood on a hassock."

"I would have doubted it. However, I suppose Angelina knows."

Never a good eater, today she ate less than usual. Her father, finishing his cold beef and salad, looked at her across the table and with a stir of misgiving thought that she looked very small and very thin. Her facial resemblance to her mother was startling—but there all similarity ended. The same dark, slanting eyes—but not laughing eyes, like her mother's. The same curving mouth, but a mouth for the most part serious. Her mother's look but his own ingrowing, in-going nature.

Not for the first time, he wondered uneasily whether he had failed in his duty towards her. A few years before, he had seen a net of prayer and priests closing round her, and had done something to restore some kind of religious balance. He had cut the last strands by arranging to send her to a Protestant school—a decision that he knew her mother would have supported. But what else had he done? He had left her too long surrounded by old women and servants—but it was too late to wish that he had set up an establishment of his own. What would have been the use of making a home for her and being obliged to leave it for 80 percent of his time? She was better off with the aunts.

He watched her as she signalled to the servant to remove her plate, on which most of the food remained untouched.

"Feeling nervous about leaving home?" he asked.

She raised her eyes to his.

"No."

"You're going to find things a bit hard at first. I'm afraid you've been brought up in luxury, and luxury's outdated. It's going to be a pretty drastic change to go to a country in which you'll have to do everything for yourself. Nobody's going to run about waiting on you."

"I don't want them to."

The light was behind him, making his hair look fair. Admiration stirred in her. His face was handsome and strong and suntanned. He was the same age as Mr. Paget—forty-three—but even the twins admitted that he looked much younger. She was proud of his looks, proud of his tall, broad figure; with the appreciation of well-cut clothes that Mademoiselle Barrault had instilled in her, she approved of his dark-gray suit. Perhaps if he had not been away so much, perhaps if, when at home, he had spent more time with her, she might have come to know him better, might have found in him someone to whom she could really talk, someone in whom perhaps she could confide.

He was looking at her speculatively, and she met his glance with her characteristic steady, unreadable gaze. What was she thinking? he wondered. He ought to know—or, not knowing, he ought to be able to guess.

"I'm sorry I'm not taking you to England," he heard himself saying, to his own surprise. And, to his greater surprise, he added: "Perhaps I'll come and fetch you home at Easter."

"Thank you."

He did not wonder at the lack of response in her tone; he was aware that he had made half-promises before and failed to keep them. Yes, he decided with a feeling of helplessness, he had undoubtedly failed in his duty. He could have arranged to spend more time in the Lisbon office, less time in foreign branches. He could have tried to get closer to her. He would have given much at this moment to be able to break through that polite, controlled, unchildlike front.

"Got all your tickets safe?" he asked.

"Yes."

"You've got a single compartment—a sleeping compartment—in

the Sud Express, and also on the night ferry, on which you'll cross the English Channel on the second night. You won't have anything to worry about. Mr. Darlan will take you to dinner tonight in the restaurant car, and then he'll see you back to your compartment. Lock your door; that long row of doors along train corridors can be very confusing, and someone might make a mistake and come in when you're asleep. You'll be asked by the attendant to give up your passport, but he'll give it back to you before you get to the French frontier."

"That's at Hendaye, isn't it?"

"Yes. When you wake up tomorrow morning, you'll probably be getting into San Sebastian. After that comes Irun, and the frontier between Spain and France. Mr. Darlan will give you lunch on the French train. You arrive at Austerlitz Station, and you have to cross Paris to get to the Gare du Nord. Mr. Darlan's sister will join you there, and the three of you will go on to England. Got all that clear?"

"Yes, thank you."

"You'll get to London—Victoria Station—early the next morning, and you'll be met by your cousin Philippa."

"I see."

The cousin's name had come up before, but he had merely said that he had written to ask her if she would meet the train at Victoria, keep Tory at her house in London for the day and night, and put her on the school train on the following morning. Tory thought it time to ask for further details.

"Is she old or young?" she enquired.

"Cousin Philippa? By your standards, old. She's about thirty-five."

"What does she look like?"

"It's more than eleven years since I saw her—she may have changed. She's . . . well, rather tall, and thin—very thin—and she's got blue eyes. There's a touch of red in her hair—or there used to be. I think you'll like her. I told you, didn't I, that she had been at the same school as the one you're going to?"

"No."

"I'm sorry. I should have done. It was remembering that fact —and of course the fact that it was a good school—that made me choose it for you."

"Is she married?"

"No." He hesitated. "She was going to be married—twice—but both times, it ... it fell through. She runs a kind of china shop—she's part owner and I think works part time."

"Is her name Brooke?"

"No. It's Brackley. Philippa Brackley. I've never traced our exact relationship; her father was a second or third cousin of my father—something like that. But after my parents died, I spent all my school holidays at her father's house in Yorkshire. He was a nice old fellow—a bit apt to go up in the air when he felt irritated, but I was very fond of him."

"Is he dead?"

"Yes. He died some years ago. Philippa was working as a secretary in London when he got ill—she gave up her job and went back to Yorkshire to nurse him. When he died, she sold the Yorkshire house and bought the one she's now in in London."

There was silence. Tory sat wondering what had gone wrong with the two engagements, leaving Miss Brackley still Miss Brackley. Then her father spoke again.

"I'm sending you to England," he told her, "because I want you to grow up in the English way. You need hardening. You need a harsher climate, a more strenuous life, less attention, more independence. I want you to grow up tough and self-reliant. When you're older, you can choose your own way of life—English or Portuguese—but you can only choose if you know both sides."

And by that time, he reflected, there might not be a choice. Portugal, for her, meant this house, in which she had been born and brought up—and by the time she was grown up it would in all probability be a convent, with Pilar and Piedade still in residence ending up as comfortably as they had begun and continued. The reckoning couldn't be long delayed; money was pouring out, most of it into the Church. Priests came and went daily; alms were showered into innumerable outstretched palms. The things of

27

great value had gone, those of less value were rapidly going. The debts were incalculable.

He watched Tory finishing her glass of milk. Then she sat waiting for his order to go and get ready to leave. Certainly, he thought, she gave no trouble. She was well guarded, but he suspected that she had her own means of escape. Thank God, she had a good brain—like his own. She found learning easy, she liked learning and she retained what she learned. She had had the run of his extensive library. Other branches of knowledge? He couldn't tell. She had friends among the servants, and there was nothing inhibited about the Portuguese peasant; she had probably picked up a lot.

The entire household assembled in the hall to see them off. Edmund endured as well as he could the tears and the lamentations and the kissing of hands, and found himself admiring his daughter's composed bearing. He hurried her out to the car, and they spoke little on the way to the station. He carried her suitcase, she carried the straw basket. He followed her into her sleeping compartment and drew from his pocket a piece of paper, which he handed to her.

"That's my travel itinerary," he told her. "It'll tell you where I am and when I'm there. I've made a rough estimate for you of the dates you should post your letters if you want to catch me anywhere."

"Thank you. When do you leave?"

"Early tomorrow morning."

"You're going to Lima, aren't you?"

"Yes." She had walked to the exit door with him, and he glanced along the platform. "Here comes Mr. Darlan."

Mr. Darlan's luggage—two large suitcases and the bag containing his golf clubs—were carried into the train and placed in his compartment, which was three doors away from Tory's. Edmund said good-bye, kissed Tory and checked that she had her passport, her tickets, her cousin Philippa's address and an adequate supply of money. Then he left the train. It began to move, and she stood watching him drift slowly away, farther and farther, until she could no longer see him.

She turned and walked along the corridor to her compartment, trying to realize that she was actually on her way. She was beginning to feel an exhilarating sense of relief, of release. For the first time in her life, she was free from Aunt Pilar's lectures and Aunt Piedade's exhortations to prayer. She was free of Mademoiselle Barrault and her repetitious views on dress, deportment and the desirability of every woman's finding a rich husband to stand between wolf and door. She was free of the nuns, with their scarcely-veiled hostility to her father. Her fetters had never hampered her unduly, but she had had to wear them. Now there was no longer any need for her to plan, to scheme, to evade. She was free—almost free. She discounted Mr. Darlan. She was aware that she had not made a favourable impression on him; apart from seeing that she ate some dinner, and perhaps checking from time to time that she had not fallen out of the train, he would probably keep to his own compartment. She did not think that she would see much of him.

Free . . .

Chapter Two

Mr. Darlan's fatherly manner was less in evidence after the train left Lisbon. He made a pretense of settling Tory into her compartment, told her that he would take her to the restaurant car for dinner and then with unconcealed relief left her to her own devices.

She took out of the basket two books and her small writing case. An examination of the food with which she had been provided proved that it was brown bread and butter with honey, and white bread and butter with ham. There were also two apples and two bananas. She ate one of the apples unpeeled and unwashed, as a salute to freedom.

In his own compartment, Mr. Darlan read the *Daily Telegraph*, put down the newspaper and reviewed his morning's activities. He could, he decided, congratulate himself. Nobody would ever again be able to accuse him of a lack of enterprise. A smile came to his lips as he thought of the congratulations to come; that carping cow, Madame Leblanc, would have to eat a good few of the insults she had levelled at him in the past. His morning's work proved that he had been right all along in urging the need to be less cautious. After years of go-slow, of hold-back, of obeying frustrating orders, how smartly he had acted today! How cleverly he had seized the golden—the adjective, so appropriate, made him laugh aloud—opportunity. Quick thinking and well-planned action; wait till Madame heard the details, wait till she saw what he had brought back. It wasn't as though he'd had time to sit down and plan the thing; it had sprung into his mind, ready-made, as soon as he had heard the discussion on the golf course. It had all been there, ready, assembled: the child in need of an escort, the child who belonged to the famous house whose treasures he had long wanted to see; he had only had to make his offer, and the rest had followed, as he had known it must: the invitation to dine, the ready assent to his request to be shown round, his first view of that fantastic chapel and what it contained . . .

Yes, there was proof enough of his ability to bring off something on his own. Soon Madame would hear the details, soon she would see what he had brought back. But he must find a way, when they met at the Gare du Nord, of getting across to her the fact that she was supposed to be his sister. Not that there was anything to fear from this mousy miss. If she saw anything beyond her neat little nose, he'd be surprised. Nice enough, in her well-drilled way, but dull; very dull. She'd have to work a lot harder when she was older, if she wanted to make an impression—although, come to think of it, there was already a hint of something attractive about her, some elusive quality—if you could spare the time to find out what it was.

His eyelids drooped. Yawning, he remembered that he had been up before dawn; never had he been so early on a job. He deserved a sleep . . .

He awoke with a feeling of heaviness, and after a time remembered Tory. Perhaps he'd better pay her a courtesy call—and after that he'd go along and see what they kept on this train in the way of drinks. He needed a drink—a long drink, a strong drink, above all a cool drink; the heating, which he had tried to turn off, was as overpowering as it had been before he fell asleep. A drink. Only one—or perhaps two. He must keep his mind clear. Not that there was any need to worry; there was only one more hurdle ahead, and with the help of Miss Mouse he would have no trouble getting over it.

He walked to Tory's compartment; her door was open and she was seated in the far corner writing a letter. He entered without ceremony and seated himself opposite her.

"Writing to your friends already?" he inquired with a ponderous effort at joviality. "Bit soon, isn't it?"

"Perhaps it is," she agreed tranquilly.

"You'll miss them, I daresay."

"Perhaps."

She had placed the writing case beside her and was sitting with her hands folded on her lap, the picture of polite attention.

"Where's this school you're going to? Not up in the frozen North, I trust? You'd feel it, you know, after living all your life in Portugal."

"It's in Sussex."

"Ah. Nice county. Had a house near the Downs, once. Done much travelling?"

"Not very much."

"At your age, I'd seen half the world—my father was a mining engineer, and where he went I went. Now I don't range much; I stick to my schedule: England in the spring, Italy in summer, Spain in the autumn, Portugal in the winter."

He paused, but she had no comment to make. Brought up as she'd been, like a princess, wouldn't you think, he asked himself irritably, that they'd have taught her to pick up and return the conversational ball? He was too hot and too thirsty to drag responses out of her.

"I'll leave you to get on with your letter," he said.

She watched him go, sighed with relief and sat looking out at the darkening countryside. When the train stopped at the spa of Luso, peasant women ranged up and down the platform selling small earthenware jars of thermal water; she leaned out and bought one and, holding it high, directed a jet of water into her mouth, a trick she had learned from Odette's Spanish lover. Cool, clear, delicious, refreshing.

Mr. Darlan was applying the same adjectives to his fourth

whiskey and soda. His self-satisfaction had become self-confidence. No longer, he promised himself, would he take orders from Madame Leblanc. He'd stuck to plan, followed the party line long enough: Lisbon, Madrid, Seville, Florence, Oporto and God knew where else. Caution, caution, caution before action had been her cry. Never had she trusted him to pull off anything on his own, never had she placed the smallest trust in him. She had accused him of a lack of nerve; in a crisis, she said, he would panic. Well, when she heard his report tomorrow, she'd realize she'd underestimated him.

Another drink? Not yet. He'd go along and tell Miss Mouse that he'd got tickets for the first dinner, and while she was washing those little patrician hands, he'd fit in another visit to the bar. But first, he'd change into a cooler shirt; this heat was getting him down.

Tory smelled the whiskey fumes as he entered her compartment. It was not an unfamiliar smell; Pilar always left out whiskey for Father Diogo or Father Arnaldo on the days on which they came to hear the Confessions of the household—and Francisco, the butler, invariably emptied the decanter when Father Diogo or Father Arnaldo departed. But Francisco's manner never lost its dignity, and he always retained the steadiness of his bearing, unlike Mr. Darlan, whose instability as he entered had not, she saw, been caused by any movement of the train. After one glance at him, she looked down at her lap and tried to forget the unlovely sight—his sparse strands of hair disarranged, his face glistening with sweat, his arms in the short-sleeved shirt looking hairy and damp and slippery.

"Ten minutes to go before dinner," he told Tory. "Feeling peckish?"

She would have given much to avoid dining with him, but she did not want to go to bed hungry. Mademoiselle Barrault, once a frequent traveller on this line, had warned her that she would get nothing but coffee and biscuits in the morning before changing to the French train.

"A little," she admitted reluctantly.

"I'll meet you in the restaurant car. It's two carriages away. Mind you don't fall off going through the joining bridges."

She decided that she would eat as fast as she could and then excuse herself and leave the table. If she kept her eyes on her plate, she wouldn't have to look at Mr. Darlan, whose appearance was becoming more and more unattractive.

Joining him at a table for two in the restaurant car, she decided that unattractive was not the word; he was repulsive. It was only by making a strong effort that she brought herself to slide into the seat opposite his. Then she gave her attention to the simple menu.

"Nothing to tempt anyone," Mr. Darlan remarked. His speech was blurred, but it held a new note of arrogance; the whiskey had reached the secret places of his mind and drowned the last vestiges of self-doubt. He no longer feared; he was scarcely interested in Madame Leblanc's reactions. Feeling as he did at this moment, he could imagine himself going along very well without her, planning his own jobs, keeping his own gains. He'd learned a lot from her, true, but now he could stand on his own feet and—what was that expression?—kick away the props. If he needed contacts, he knew other women as clever as she was, and a good deal more attractive. Not that he went after women, he mused with a touch of smugness; offer him Scotch or sex and his hand would reach out for the bottle. Give him whiskey and you could keep the women. But he had to watch his intake. No more drinks tonight. He'd had too many already, and what if they began to loosen his tongue? What would this child say if he . . .

Child? For the first time, he looked at her with attention. Focusing was becoming difficult, and perhaps it was this slightly hazy view that made her look, suddenly, a woman. The rose-shaded lamp threw a soft circle round her, and within it she sat motionless. She had not spoken since she took her seat, and she did not appear to have heard some casual remarks he had made to her—but he was no longer looking for response. He was watching the slow lift of her eyelids and the unveiling of her dark, unreadable eyes. He studied the perfect oval of her face, the clear, flawless skin, the curve of cheek, the long, thick lashes. Her hair, straight, silky, fell to her shoulders, the ends curling inward and upward. The more he looked, the more he marvelled at his early failure to have noted the signs of beauty. The high cheekbones and the slant of her eyes he attributed to some probably Chinese strain in her ancestry—hadn't he been told that her grandfather came from Macau? That would account, too, for her unchildlike capacity for repose, the inscrutability of her glance, the total lack of give-away.

How, he wondered, could her father have continued to regard her as a child? Those old women, her great-aunts, would of course see nothing but her small, undeveloped body—but her father? He was in his way as unforthcoming as the child was, but he was a man of the world; how could he have failed to see or to sense this potential, this powerhouse? Perhaps he had seen. Perhaps that was why she was on her way to a cooling establishment. Perhaps he thought or hoped or believed that an English school would slow down the maturing process.

He had ordered food and it had been brought and the remnants of his reason told him that he ought to eat in order to counteract the effects of the drinks he had had—but he had no appetite. He wanted to go on looking at her. He did not want to talk. He was afraid to talk, afraid that he would say too much and give away his reason for offering to travel with her. It was safer to keep his mouth shut.

Tory welcomed the silence. She knew that drink acted in different ways on different people. It excited some, it depressed others; on Odette's lover it had a tearful effect. Some drunk people talked, others grew morose. Mr. Darlan could obviously be placed in this last category. While he was feeling morose, she could enjoy her soup—true Portuguese vegetable soup—and the fish and chicken that followed. She had no room for *pudim flan*, the caramel custard that was the almost inevitable end to all Portuguese dinners; instead, she took an apple from the tray of fruit that the waiter brought round, and began to peel it. And as she did so, she felt Mr. Darlan's hand touching hers.

She drew back her hand. She did not think that she had been responsible for the brief contact, but she murmured an apology.

The waiter returned to offer coffee. For one only? He withdrew, and as he turned away, Mr. Darlan's hand came forward and closed tightly over one of hers.

She threw a swift glance across the table. He met it with a look that he tried in vain to make paternal. She attempted to withdraw her hand, found it imprisoned in his close, moist clasp and for a few moments sat fighting a sick feeling of repugnance and disgust. Then all other emotions were swamped in a wave of fury which almost engulfed her. She raised her eyes fully and took in the picture opposite: a balding head, a bull neck rising out of a pseudo-cowboy, sweat-stained shirt; a round, puffy face gleaming with perspiration—and a large, hairy hand, like some revolting sea creature, clasping her own. This was the man who had dared to touch her. This drunken, repulsive old man had grasped her hand with his. Trusted by her father to see her safely to England, he had soaked himself in whiskey and shed the disguise he had worn in Portugal.

Exerting all her strength, she freed her hand. She found herself on her feet; she heard herself thanking him for the dinner and wishing him a calm good-night. She brushed past the waiter who had come to serve the coffee and made her way out of the restaurant car, and went as swiftly as she could along the corridors of the swaying train, pushing past fellow-passengers, bumping against windows as the train lurched. It was not easy to find her compartment—the row stretched endlessly, confusingly—but at last she reached it and went in and locked the door behind her. Then she stood listening, steadying herself against the bed, which the attendant had made up during her absence. After a time she drew a deep breath of relief; there was no sign, no sound from Mr. Darlan.

She sat on the bed and took stock of the situation. She had no hope of shaking him off; he would be with her all the way to London. There was no fear in her mind as she contemplated the day and night that remained of the journey; all she had to do was keep out of reach of any further drunken fumblings, but the thought of having to set eyes on him again filled her with loathing.

She could almost smile as she remembered the anxious inquiries made by her aunts to assure themselves that he was a suitable escort and protector. They should have plied him with Father Diogo's whiskey, and then they would have found out what kind of man he really was.

But she was here in her compartment, locked in, safe from him, and nothing would induce her to leave it again until the morning. She began to regret having come back so fast from the restaurant car—she should have made a stop at one of the lavatories. But she wasn't going out again; he might be standing in the corridor, waiting for her. And surely . . . hadn't Mademoiselle Barrault told her about the toilet arrangements in the sleeping compartments, and wasn't there something provided . . .

She investigated. Yes, there was. In the cupboard below the washbasin she discovered a heavy china utensil shaped like an outsize sauceboat. The prospect of using it in a train that was dancing like this one made the thought of Mr. Darlan fade from her mind. By the time she had given herself one of the sponge baths recommended by Mademoiselle Barrault, cleaned her teeth, said her Protestant prayers, made an examination of all the light switches and got into bed, she had almost forgotten him.

Morning brought remembrance, and a renewed determination to keep as far away from him as possible. She raised the blind and looked out the window; this must still be Spain, and presumably they would soon be at Irun. She washed and dressed and opened the door of the compartment; the attendant passing with a pile of used bed linen paused to answer her questions. They were running twenty minutes late; they would be at Irun in an hour; could he bring her coffee?

He brought it—doubtful coffee in a plastic cup, already sweetened, with two biscuits in a little packet. She shut herself in, drank as much as she could and poured the rest away into the basin. Then she went into the corridor and stood waiting as the attendant tidied the compartment. As he came out, she gave him the sum of money her father had told her to give him, and then went into the compartment and completed her packing.

The train stopped: Irun. There was nothing to see but a narrow platform and passengers disembarking, but there was an air of bustle, a feeling of frontier.

She did not see Mr. Darlan until the train had crossed into France and was slowing to a halt. He appeared at the door of her compartment, looking gray-faced and haggard, wearing the suit in which he had left Lisbon and a warm overcoat. In his hand was a bundle, which she recognized as the shirt he had changed into the evening before.

"Good morning." He spoke curtly. "I'm going to shove this shirt into that basket of yours for the moment. Can't fit it. I'll take it back as soon as we're in the other train."

He had not waited for permission; he had reached over and taken the basket and pushed in the bundle, and she told herself that it would be not only easy but a pleasure, as she carried the basket along the crowded platform, to let the shirt slip out. Then she saw that there would be no hope of doing anything of the kind, for Mr. Darlan grasped the basket and, leaving her to bring her suitcase, went back to his own compartment.

"Got to get a move on," he called over his shoulder. "I've got to see about getting a seat on the train; I didn't have time to book."

By the time she had put on her overcoat and beret and gloves and walked down the corridor to join him, she saw that he had let down the window of his compartment and was handing out his two suitcases and his golf bag to a porter. She handed out her own case. Outside waited a gray, bitterly cold morning, with a cutting wind. Two thoughts came simultaneously: that a woolly, long-sleeved undergarment would be a great help in keeping out the cold . . . and that she would rather die of cold than wear one.

She followed Mr. Darlan on to the platform.

"If you've left anything behind, you've lost it," he told Tory. "I'm not going back through this crowd."

He spoke irritably. His head was throbbing, and the half-cold coffee the attendant had brought him had done nothing to relieve the weight that pressed on his eyes. His recollection of the previous night was dim. He had drunk too much—of that the hammer blows inside his head were proof—but had he said anything indiscreet, given anything away? No; impossible. The girl looked just the same, which she couldn't have done if he'd let out even a hint of the truth. He recalled vaguely his impressions during dinner—hadn't he patted her hand? If he had, it would have looked like a fatherly touch. Where the devil was she? Where had she got to? It was absolutely essential that they go through the customs side by side.

Tory was some distance away. She had fallen behind and found herself in the midst of a crowd of Portuguese immigrants on their way to work in France. Many of them were accompanied by their families, and she was feeling very much at home. She was surprised to hear a loudspeaker giving out notices not in French but in Portuguese: would all Portuguese, it warned, be wary of their purses and their persons; would they refrain from involving themselves with strangers and would they above all refuse to hand over money or to accompany strangers who approached them with any proposition, however attractive-sounding. The crowd round her, for the most part simple peasants looking dazed and helpless, told her how necessary such warnings must be. There were women carrying their worldly possessions in bundles on their heads, old men clutching swollen sacks, children carrying baskets of food. Some of the women were swathed in the thick, hand-knitted shawls of Portugal, others wore the traditional costume of their region, or coats that looked pitifully inadequate to keep out the bitter cold. Borne along on the stream, Tory forgot Mr. Darlan until she felt her arm seized and saw his angry, anxious face close to her own.

"Keep close to me going through the Customs," he ordered. "If they ask you, all you have to say is that you've nothing to declare."

They reached the line of Customs officials. Mr. Darlan lifted onto the counter the three suitcases and his golf bag, and in front of Tory placed the basket he had been carrying. To her shame, she saw protruding from it the collar of his soiled shirt and two black-spotted bananas; she was not surprised at the Customs official's look of distaste. To his look of inquiry, she acknowledged reluctantly that she was the owner of the basket; he nodded, chalked it and her suitcase and turned his attention to Mr. Darlan, motioning him to open the larger of the two suitcases. Mr. Darlan took out a bunch of keys, selected one and opened the case and Tory glanced at its contents: a bulky dressing gown, a pair of black shoes in a plastic bag, some paperback books, a wide-brimmed hat packed upside down, a black-bound book, socks and handkerchiefs—all of them occupying not more than half the space inside the suitcase. He could, she noted indignantly, have made room for a dozen shirts if he had wanted to; he had used her basket simply to save himself the trouble of opening his case.

The examination was brief, the luggage was chalked and they moved on.

"That's that." Mr. Darlan's voice, as he handed the heavier luggage into the care of a porter, expressed deep relief. "We're through. Now we'll see about my seat on the train. Doesn't look as though there'll be much difficulty at the first-class end."

The corridor of the Paris train was wider than the one they had just left, but there was the same confusing line of compartments stretching from one end of the carriage to the other. They found Tory's booked seat in an otherwise empty compartment; Mr. Darlan's cases and golf bag were swung onto the rack and Tory's case placed beside them. She put out her hand to take the basket, but Mr. Darlan placed it beside his suitcases.

"I'll let you have it once the train gets going," he said. "Don't touch it yet—I wrapped a bottle of shaving lotion into the shirt, and I don't want it broken."

His tone was brusque. He took his seat in a corner and put his feet up on the seat opposite, bundling his overcoat into a pillow for his head. The thought of passing the whole day in his company gave Tory a feeling of nausea.

A hope that she might be spared this rose as she recognized a party of skiers going past the compartment, their ski boots pounding on the carpeted stretch of corridor. They were a French family named Cruzon, and the only daughter, Monique, had been a classmate of hers at the convent. If they were going to be on the train . . .

"Only as far as Bayonne," Monique told her, to her disappointment, when she had caught up with her in the corridor. "Then we get off."

"I didn't see you on the train last night."

"We didn't have sleepers." They spoke in French. "We passed the night sitting up. My father forgot to make reservations. Come and talk to me."

The family had settled into the compartment next door to the one occupied by Mr. Darlan and Tory. The settling in had not been accomplished without difficulty; Monsieur Cruzon was not travelling, and his wife was coping with Monique and four younger brothers, none of whom showed any disposition to be helpful.

"They are overtired," the exhausted Madame Cruzon explained to Tory. "All night without a bed, it was too bad, they are not accustomed to it. They didn't sleep, so naturally I didn't sleep. Only Monique slept. And since this morning the boys have been devils, devils. Thank God my brother is to meet us at Bayonne; that at least will be something. Look at them."

Tory looked. She had seen them before on many occasions and had earned a certain measure of respect by her ability to give as good as she got. Their ages were eight, seven, six and five, and they were uniformly undersized, wiry and incredibly tough. The youngest, Jean-Paul, was hanging from the luggage rack. The brother next in age, Ugo, was lying along it. The other two boys, Claud and Patrice, were rolling on the floor between the seats, fighting over a toy trumpet. Claud won, and proceeded to give a solo performance that echoed down the corridor.

"You are only going as far as Bayonne?" Tory asked Madame Cruzon.

"Yes, but after Bayonne, there is more—much more. We have to change to another train and go as far as Pau, and then another train to Lourdes and then two hours in a bus up to the mountains. Two hours . . . can you imagine how these boys will behave? In daylight, they would be able to see the mountains and that would keep them quiet, but it will be dark and there will be nothing to see.

And they will be sick in the bus. Every year we make this journey, every year my husband forgets to book sleeping compartments, every year the boys are sick in the bus."

Tory had paid very little attention to this travelogue. She had been doing some calculations, and she now decided that the company of even so wild a quartet as the Cruzon boys would be preferable to being alone with Mr. Darlan.

"There are free seats in the compartment next to yours—the one I'm travelling in," she told Madame Cruzon. "If you will send the boys in when the train starts, I will read to them and keep them quiet."

Madame Cruzon looked down at her in amazed gratitude.

"You would not mind doing that?" she asked.

"You will be able to get some rest," Tory said. "It's a pity," she added with sincerity, "that you're only going to Bayonne."

She went back to her compartment and seated herself in a corner. Mr. Darlan's eyes were closed; he appeared to be asleep. As soon as the train began to move, Monique and her brothers streamed in from next door, carrying books. Mr. Darlan opened his eyes and after one incredulous look ordered them, in fluent French, to leave at once. By way of answer, Claud clambered onto the seat beside him, one of his ski boots dealing Mr. Darlan a sharp crack on the knee.

"Begin, Tory," ordered Ugo. "Read *Mille Fleurs* and—"

"No!" yelled Patrice. "Not that. Read from the red book."

"Not the red book," shouted Ugo. "I'm going to choose."

Mr. Darlan, his face working with fury, got up, left the compartment and took up a position in the corridor. Tory opened the blue book and began to read aloud; one by one, the boys gave the story their attention and settled down to listen. Mr. Darlan did not return. Madame Cruzon, in the neighbouring compartment, snatched some much-needed sleep.

Bayonne was reached, in Tory's opinion, far too soon. Monique and her brothers said good-bye, joined the grateful Madame Cruzon and lowered their window to pass their luggage out to a porter. Mr. Darlan, looking sick and yellow, came in from the corridor.

"I've got a headache," he understated. "I'm going out to see if I can buy something to relieve it." He half turned to go and then paused to point to Tory's basket on the rack. "Don't touch that," he warned. "I'll clear my things out of it when I come back."

He need not have asked her not to touch it. One sleeve of the shirt, dislodged by the shaking of the train, had slipped out and was hanging over the side of the luggage rack; under the arm was visible a large sweat stain. She walked down the corridor to the exit door and stood watching the Cruzons helping to place their luggage on the porter's wagon. Farther down the platform, outside the third-class carriages, she could see groups of Portuguese immigrants standing by the doors, buying coffee from a station barrow. She waved good-bye to the Cruzons and went back to the compartment she shared with Mr. Darlan. Standing at the door, she stared in, seeing in her mind his face, badly shaved, mottled, with bag-encircled eyes, and wished with all her heart that she could have been alone. There were people in the compartments farther up and down the corridor, but nobody had taken the places vacated by the Cruzons and nobody had taken the vacant seats in this one. Mr. Darlan would come back, would sit opposite her all day, would take her to lunch in the restaurant car . . .

If only, she thought yearningly, she could be free of him! If only she could remove his luggage and place it next door, as a sort of hint. But it was hopeless for her to try to lift his heavy cases. Wasn't there anything she could do? She closed her eyes. If only she could think . . . think . . .

She opened her eyes. She couldn't lift his things, but she could lift her own. She would move to the next-door compartment, and when he returned she would explain that, as he had a bad headache, she thought he might prefer to be alone. Or if that sounded unconvincing, she could invent a headache of her own—he didn't have a monopoly in headaches.

Without further hesitation, she lifted down her suitcase and then reached up for the basket. Its weight astonished her, but she had no time to wonder; she carried both pieces of luggage into the compartment next door. She returned to detach the slip of paper that had marked her booked seat, and fastened it to the corresponding seat next door. The window, opened when the Cruzons were handing out their luggage, had not been closed; she decided not to close it until the train was moving.

She stood in the corridor and stared out at the other side of the station, watching a departing train and planning what she would say to Mr. Darlan when he returned. He might be surprised, she thought, but he would probably welcome being alone as much as she did.

She saw him walking down the corridor towards her, and prepared her explanation: very sorry, headache, might be trainsick, much better be alone. But no explanation was asked for. Mr. Darlan stopped at the door and she heard him give a loud exclamation. She turned and saw that his eyes were going in panic round the open-windowed compartment. He spoke in a choked voice.

"My luggage! My God, my luggage! Who's taken it?"

Tory stared at him in amazement—and then she realized that he imagined himself to be in the compartment in which they had travelled from Hendaye. Uncertain how to meet this unexpected development, she played for time.

"Your luggage?" she said.

"My God, yes. Have you been at this door all the time I've been away?"

"No."

"Then . . . then . . . "

He was at the window, leaning out. Over his bowed body she could see, some distance away, the wagon on which the luggage of the French family had been placed. It was being wheeled towards the exit; from its sides protruded something that she knew to be skis but that to a man half-blinded by headache might look like a golf bag.

"There it is! They've . . . Hey! Come back, you!"

Shouting, in French as well as in English, was no use. The wagon, the Cruzons following it, went on its way. Mr. Darlan gave another hoarse shout and seemed about to hurl himself through the window; then he turned, lurched through the compartment, pushed past Tory and ran rapidly back the way he had come. She walked forward and stood at the open window and in a moment saw him emerge from the train and go in pursuit of the wagon, running, stumbling, recovering and all the while shouting. The wagon disappeared into a building; Mr. Darlan went after it. And at the same moment the train began smoothly, imperceptibly, to move. It had gathered momentum before she saw Mr. Darlan reappear and take some uncertain steps in its wake; then, realizing that it was hopeless to get aboard, he stopped and gave a gesture of despair. The train carried her beyond the point at which she could see him.

She closed the window and sat trying to realize what had happened. Mr. Darlan had thought that the Cruzons had mistakenly put his luggage on to the wagon with their own. He had rushed out of the train and it had started without him. For a moment she felt sympathy—and then she remembered that what was bad luck for Mr. Darlan was good luck for herself. She was alone. With some more good luck, she could avoid the sister who was waiting at the Gare du Nord, and go all the way to England by herself. She felt no nervousness at the prospect; she had complete confidence in her ability to look after herself. Quiet, polite as was her manner, the circumstances of her upbringing had given her the habit of authority. She was accustomed to ask for and to receive service; if no service was available, she had no doubt that she could manage without it. To travel alone held nothing but excitement; to travel without Mr. Darlan gave the last touch of bliss.

The train sped on, and France opened before her. Snow began to fall; she had seen snow lying on mountaintops, but never had she seen these flakes softly falling, gently descending and spreading a white carpet over the countryside. Again and again she wiped the mist from the window and pressed her face to the pane to gaze out at the entrancing scene.

After a time, hunger brought her to the thought of lunch. An attendant came round offering tickets, but she shook her head; she did not want to eat lunch alone, and she knew where she could find congenial company: she would make her way down to the third-class carriages and join the Portuguese immigrants. She knew that she would be welcome among them, and she looked forward to exchanging her sandwiches for a slice of dark-textured, homemade bread and a few slices of *chouriço*.

But first, there was Mr. Darlan's shirt to get rid of. She could not decide what to do with it—leave it next door, on top of one of his suitcases? Leave it in this compartment? Throw it out of the window? That seemed a waste; there were men in those carriages she was going to who would welcome a shirt, even if it wasn't a warm shirt or a clean shirt. She would fold it up—the prospect was not pleasant—and give to any Portuguese who wanted it.

She reached up to lift down the basket; once again, its weight amazed her. Sitting down, she took out the bundled shirt and, remembering Mr. Darlan's warning about a bottle of shaving lotion, unwrapped the bundle carefully. One layer, and then another—and another. And then the object that had been wrapped inside it came to view. It was not a bottle of shaving lotion.

It was the golden statuette of Saint Christopher.

Chapter Three

A thief. She made a swift, instinctive movement to hide the statuette from the gaze of people passing the compartment. Mr. Darlan was a thief. He had stolen Saint Christopher from the chapel.

When? How? She did not know when or how, but she understood well enough that she had been used as a cover to get the statuette past the Customs at Hendaye. He had calculated, rightly, that a basket belonging to a child, a schoolgirl, a basket with a soiled shirt and some stale fruit in it, was not likely to arouse suspicion in the mind of a Customs official. He had used her luggage, used her as a screen. It was for this that he had offered to accompany her to England.

And this sister who was waiting for him in Paris—was she, too, a thief? If not, did she know that her brother was a thief? Had he told her that he was travelling with a valuable gold statuette? Did he plan to leave Saint Christopher with her in France, or had he intended to take it to England?

In Lisbon, they were searching for the statuette and blaming Jesuina. A thief, and a liar who had deceived her father and her aunts. And he had rushed out of the train at Bayonne to recover what he thought was his luggage because that, too, doubtless contained more stolen items. From the Casa Fenix? She thought it unlikely. Nothing else had been missing from the chapel, and only in the chapel was there much, lately, to tempt a thief.

If he had not lost the train at Bayonne, she would have been in his company throughout today, not knowing what he was, not knowing what he had hidden in her basket. But he had gone—and she had Saint Christopher. That was all that mattered.

Having got it, what was she to do with it? It was impossible to take it to school with her. Would there be any place in the house of this cousin, any safe, secret place in which she could hide it while she was away at school? She was to stay at the house for one night before returning to Portugal for the Easter holidays—could she find a hiding place for the statuette until then? She anticipated no trouble about getting it back to Portugal in her luggage; so much, at least, Mr. Darlan had taught her.

The thought of informing an unknown cousin of what had occurred did not stay for more than a moment in her mind. The circumstances of the journey were too unlikely, too fantastic to be believed. If she showed the statuette to Philippa Brackley and told her that it had been hidden in Mr. Darlan's shirt, would she, would anyone else believe the story? Only people who knew her would know that she was speaking the truth. She would write to her father and tell him that Saint Christopher was safe, and he could decide how to get the news to the aunts. But apart from telling her father, she would say nothing. Mr. Darlan was a thief and she hoped that one day he would be found out and put into prison, but she did not believe that any charges she might make against him would be taken seriously. The police would have to be told, and the police were all very well if you wanted them to recover your stolen property, but in this case there was nothing to recover and there would be nothing for the police to do but ask questions and disbelieve her answers. Had she seen Mr. Darlan take the statuette from the chapel? No. Had she seen it in his possession? No. Had she seen him wrap it in the checked sports shirt? No and no and no.

She sat with the saint hidden on her lap, staring out unseeingly at the snow-covered landscape and struggling against an uncharacteristic feeling of depression. This was the first real crisis of her life, and there was nobody to whom she could turn for help. Her father was in Lima, or on his way there, as far away in body as he had always been in spirit. Her aunts, Mademoiselle Barrault . . . she could not reach them, and even if she had been able to they would have been useless.

She got up and opened her suitcase. Into it she put the statuette, wrapped in one of the long-sleeved woollen garments. She folded the checked shirt, handling it gingerly and with loathing, and put in into the basket. Then, carrying both pieces of luggage, she left the compartment—for good; she did not intend to return to it. As she passed the next-door compartment, she glanced up at Mr. Darlan's two suitcases and golf bag, still neatly aligned on the luggage rack. They would be found when the train reached Paris and perhaps opened before Mr. Darlan came to claim them, and more stolen goods might be discovered in them. And yet . . . if they contained stolen goods, why had he been so ready to open his suitcase for inspection at Hendaye? And if they didn't contain stolen goods, why had he rushed out of the train in a panic in pursuit of them?

She didn't know. She would probably never know. She had the statuette and that was all she cared about. The first shock of discovery had passed; already she was doing her best to put Mr. Darlan out of her mind until it became necessary—if it ever did—to recall him.

It seemed a very long way to the third-class carriages—corridor after corridor with clattering, swaying bridges linking them. She found movement difficult with no free hand to steady herself. But at last she entered a corridor and smelled the familiar kitchen smells of home: garlic and oranges, highly spiced sausages and above all the unmistakable odour of salted cod, the *bacalhau* that every family party without exception was carrying to the relatives awaiting them in Paris.

She stopped at the first open door, and looked in. For a few moments, unnoticed, she was able to study the occupants of the overcrowded compartment: a well-dressed young man whom she guessed to be an immigrant who had prospered in France and was now taking his family back with him. In the middle seats were his wife, his parents and his four young children; in the far corners were his grandparents, huddled in shawls in spite of the stifling atmosphere, eating bread spread with cold omelette. The young wife was distributing food to the children, two of whom were on the seat and two on the floor. The young man was opening a bottle of wine. He was the first to catch sight of Tory, and his sudden stillness brought the eyes of all the others to rest on her. She spoke in their language.

"I travelled from Lisbon in the care of a friend of my father," she said, "but unhappily, he got out of the train at Bayonne and was left behind. I have food with me, but I felt homesick and so I came to listen to some Portuguese."

Before the last sentence had ended, the family had sprung into action. The two youngest children were swept up and thrust onto the laps of their grandparents. The other two were telescoped into a huddle next to the old man. The middle-aged woman, perspiring in a heavy skirt and blouse, banged the free space on the seat violently and then dusted it with her husband's hat. The open baskets of food on the floor were pushed aside; Tory was invited to come in and make herself comfortable.

She entered thankfully and took the place offered. If they knew Lisbon at all, she thought it probable that they would have heard of the Casa Fenix, and might even know one or more of the servants who worked there. And so it proved. Before she had received her share of food, familiar names were being tossed from one to the other in the compartment.

When the train slowed down on the outskirts of Paris, Tory offered Mr. Darlan's shirt, neatly folded, to the old man. The owner, she explained, had left it behind on the train when he got off. The truth. Grandfather opened the shirt, examined it, held it against him for size, folded it up again and, expressing his thanks, thrust it into the sack that held his belongings.

Before she left the train at Austerlitz, Tory tried to return good for good by guarding the older members of the family and the children, while the young man and his wife went in search of the friends who had promised to meet them. Then she made her farewells, refused offers of help or company and went her way alone, carrying her two pieces of luggage. There were some hours to wait before catching the night train from the Gare du Nord; if it had been daylight, she would have made a bargain with a taxi driver to take her on a brief sight-seeing tour of the city—but it was too dark to admire anything except the lights, and she decided that she would spend the intervening hours here at Austerlitz. She would buy a book and read, and before leaving for the Gare du Nord, she would buy some sandwiches at the buffet and eat them as her dinner on the night train.

But the first necessity was a wash to remove the grime of the train; a splash in a full-sized basin, with hot and cold water gushing from the taps. She found the cloakroom, placed her luggage on a chair at the end of a row of basins and, filling a basin almost to the top, leaned over and splashed her face, disregarding the overflow on her hair and her clothes. She took out the hand towel that Mademoiselle Barrault had put into the basket, dried herself and combed her hair. With a change of blouse, she felt fresh again.

Folding the towel to replace it in the basket, she hesitated. The statuette had greatly increased the weight of her suitcase; why carry two things when one would do? She emptied the basket, put everything it contained into her suitcase, closed and locked it and swung it to the ground. The empty basket she left on a chair, which she pushed out of sight behind the row of basins. Then she picked up her case and walked out onto the station platform, which seemed quiet and empty in comparison with the tumult and bustle of her arrival.

She allowed herself ample time to transfer from station to station, and arrived at the Gare du Nord with fifteen minutes to spare. She walked slowly beside the train looking for the number of her coach, passing groups of passengers standing at the doors. She had found her carriage and was about to climb into it when a voice behind her spoke sharply.

"You. Little girl."

She turned to find herself facing a woman of about forty wearing a black coat and a small black felt hat and carrying a very large handbag. She had spoken English with a strong French accent.

"Did you come today from Lisbon?" she asked Tory in the same tone.

"Yes."

"I am looking for someone about your age who ... Do you speak French?"

"Yes."

"You came today from Hendaye?" the woman went on in French.

"Yes."

"First from Lisbon on the Sud Express?"

"Yes."

"What is your name?"

"Vitorina Brooke."

"My God!" Fury, until now held in check, was released in the exclamation. "My God, the time I've wasted looking for you. Not only here. At Austerlitz, too. Hours, first there and then here. How was it that I missed you when you got off the train at Austerlitz?"

Tory thought it possible that it was because she had been hidden from view by grandfather and grandmother and the children—but she did not say so. There was obviously more to come.

"My name is Madame Leblanc. Today, Mr. Darlan telephoned to me from Bayonne and said that I must go to meet you at Austerlitz. He had lost the train, lost his luggage, lost God knows what. Principally, it was clear to me that what he had lost was his head. Why, in the first place, did he get off the train?"

"He had a headache. He went to buy something to make it better."

"But why did he take his luggage? This is what I could not understand in his explanation. Why, why, why did he take his luggage with him?"

"He didn't."

"He told me that it had gone. Can luggage go by itself? There is something here that I do not understand. Tell me exactly what happened. You left Lisbon with Mr. Darlan?"

"Yes. He told my father that we were going to meet his sister—Mr. Darlan's sister—at the Gare du Nord and go on to England with her."

"His sister? Oh, his *sister*. Yes, yes, yes; go on."

The moment of blank bewilderment had told Tory that whoever Madame Leblanc was, she was not Mr. Darlan's sister. She went on speaking calmly.

"We changed this morning into the French train at Hendaye."

"And at Bayonne, he got out of the train?"

"Yes. And when he came back, he said his luggage was missing, because it wasn't on the luggage rack."

"But you were there, still on the train. If his luggage had been taken away, you must have seen something. You said nothing, made no inquiry as to why somebody was removing it?"

"I wasn't in the compartment all the time—I was at the door at the end. When I went back, I stood looking out on the other side, not the platform side. The window in the compartment was open."

"Who opened it—you?"

"No."

"And when Mr. Darlan found that his luggage was missing, what did he do?"

"He leaned out of the window and shouted to a porter who was wheeling a wagon with some luggage on it, and then he ran out of the train and tried to stop the porter, but he couldn't. Then the train began to move and Mr. Darlan was left behind."

"The fool, the crazy fool!" There was undiluted bitterness in Madame Leblanc's tone. "This I always feared. I still do not understand everything, but in one thing I was right: that he lost his head." She stared down at Tory, her eyes narrowing until they were two slits of suspicion. "But he told me that he had given some of his luggage to you. He put it into a basket that you had. He said that I must go to Austerlitz to get it. I see no basket."

"I did have one," Tory said. "When we got to Hendaye this morning, Mr. Darlan put a shirt into it."

"A shirt?"

53

"He bundled it up and said he couldn't fit it into his own luggage, but he told me not to touch it because he'd wrapped a bottle of shaving lotion in it and he said—"

"I do not wish to hear what he said. He is a liar. I am not his sister and there was no intention that I should go to England with you or with him. Where is the basket?"

"I left it behind at Austerlitz."

There was a pause. Then Madame Leblanc spoke with difficulty.

"You . . . *what* did you say?"

"I wanted to have a wash, so I went into the cloakroom at Austerlitz, and when I came out, I left the basket behind."

"My God! Where? Where? Where?"

"On a chair near the basin I had a wash in."

"You are quite certain, you are absolutely certain that it was in the cloakroom you left it, and not on the train?"

"Yes, quite certain. It was—"

She stopped. Madame Leblanc had turned away and was walking with short, hurried, agitated steps and then—the last Tory was ever to see of her—breaking into a trot. Climbing onto the train, she told herself that good luck had indeed been with her on the journey. Mr. Darlan had gone. His supposed sister had gone —and if she had gone to Austerlitz, she would find that she had wasted her time. She had said that she had not intended to go to England, which probably meant that Saint Christopher wouldn't have gone either. That was a very large bag she had been carrying, quite large enough to hide something in, for instance a gold statuette. But Saint Christopher wasn't in her bag. He was safe in the suitcase, and there was nothing to worry about now except how to get him back to his place in the chapel. She had been in the company of two crooks, but they had been left behind and she was in a warm train with a compartment of her own, about to cross the English Channel for the first time. And on the other side was England, and before getting to England there would be another Customs examination, but the attendant had told her that this would take place on the train and he did not think anybody would bother her. Just in case, she would take Saint Christopher out of the suitcase and put him carefully into the pocket of her coat and hang it up, and she'd be surprised if anybody thought of looking there.

Nobody did. She had intended to stay awake until the train reached the coast, being anxious to find out how the business of getting the train onto the ferry was accomplished, but she fell asleep as soon as she lay down on her berth, and did not wake until the attendant was moving along the corridor on the following morning, knocking on the doors of still-sleeping passengers and announcing that the train would arrive at Victoria in twenty minutes.

She got up, washed and dressed and put the statuette back into her suitcase. As she closed and locked it, the train began to slow down, and she went to the window to look out. She was here. This was London and this was her native land, though she didn't feel particularly English, didn't in fact feel particularly anything. She had arrived, and there was an unknown cousin waiting for her, and it was silly to be sorry that the journey was over, because it had to end some time and she had been lucky to enjoy so much of it without disagreeable attachments. The future did not seem very bright; the possession of the statuette weighed heavily on her mind. Apart from that, there was a long day to be spent thinking of something to say to a stranger, and then there would be the night, and tomorrow there would be a school train and a crowd of girls and teachers and Attention, Girls, Please, and Kindly Answer When Your Name Is Called, and no more friendly babel of languages—just English, and they'd be certain to comment on hers, which her father had told her had certain un-English inflections. Then school. She wouldn't mind the lessons, but it wasn't going to be all learning. It would also be competitive games, which she loathed, teams and matches and Play Up the Home Side, and no hope of getting away at the day's end, as she had been able to do at the convent.

It was no use delaying. She must get off the train, and then How do you do, Are you Miss Brackley, It's very kind of you to meet me and see me off to school. No, Mr. Darlan only came as far as Bayonne and his sister didn't come at all.

She was so busy rehearsing phrases that it was some time before she realized that there was nobody to address them to. The crowd had streamed out of the train, streamed away, leaving only a trickle of passengers. There had been people meeting other people, people anxiously scanning the faces of the newly arrived, but nobody had given her so much as a glance, and she could see nobody in the distance who looked as though they were coming to meet her.

After a time, she looked at her watch: fifteen minutes since the train had arrived. She was by now almost alone on the platform. She found a bench and sat down. After five more minutes, she took out her writing case and found the address her father had written in it: 14 Elcombe Grove. Should she get into a taxi and go there? Suppose her cousin wasn't there? She couldn't stand on the doorstep. She was cold and hungry—never in her life did she remember thinking with such longing about food. She had money; she could go and eat breakfast in the station buffet, but if she did that and her cousin arrived, they'd miss one another.

She saw a woman approaching and sat watching her, and as the figure drew nearer she found herself hoping very much that this would prove to be her cousin. She would like a cousin like this. But this wasn't the one. Her father had said that her cousin was thin, and this one was fat, or perhaps not fat but nicely rounded. A beautiful coat in a soft shade of green, a fur hood encircling a face with a very clear skin. A small nose. Eyes—not near enough to see their colour—yes, a lovely shade of deep blue, with dark lashes.

But it wasn't her cousin. Without a look, without a glance, the vision swept by, and Tory, dazed with disappointment and cold and emptiness, watched her go. She was unsought and, as far as she could make out, unwanted. To be unwanted was a new and unwelcome sensation. Whatever had been the drawbacks of life at the Casa Fenix, she had never been in any danger of being forgotten. The over-attention that had smothered her and that she had spent so much time avoiding now seemed to her an almost desirable state. England appeared to her a very cold and unfriendly country; she was sitting here unmet, alone.

Not alone. The lady in the fur hood had returned and was seated on the bench beside her. She had opened her handbag and was taking out a small diary. Going through its pages, she found the one she wanted.

"Victoria Station, nine A.M." she read aloud, and, turning to Tory, continued without pause. "This is Victoria and it's only about half past nine, which of course is late, but not so late that they'd give up and go away. But they did, which I must say was rather precipitate, don't you think so? If they've rushed off to my house, they're going to find it's not the slightest use battering on the door, because I'm not there—I'm here. What time do you make it?"

"Half past nine."

"That's what I said." Her voice was very clear and very musical; she spoke quickly, but with calmness. "I daresay it seemed to them a long wait, but I do think they might have stuck it out. Look how patiently you're sitting here—*you* haven't rushed off, and very sensible, too. When your relations come to look for you, here you'll be, all ready to be picked up and taken away. You look French—are you?"

"No. I—"

"Not? I would have put money on it. Spanish?"

"No. English. I—"

"Then where did you come from?"

"From Portugal."

The blue eyes opened wider. There was a pause, and Tory waited anxiously; she wanted the lovely, lilting voice to go on and on. She was so nice, she looked so nice, she sounded so nice, what a pity, what a terrible pity she hadn't turned out to be Cousin Philippa.

"All by yourself? I think that shows great initiative, or do I mean enterprise? But you look a very sensible little thing who knows how to take care of herself without any fuss or bother. I came to meet someone about your age. I suppose I'd better go home and see what they've done with her." She rose and stood looking down at Tory, whose heart sank into her new school shoes. Then, to Tory's infinite relief, the lady sat down again. "Come to think of it, I don't like to go away and leave you sitting here like this, all alone. Can't we go and telephone to your mother or your aunt or whoever it is who's left you in the lurch in this disgraceful way? What's their name?"

"My name's Vitorina Brooke. I came—"

She stopped. The lady was regarding her with eyes opened to their widest extent. She spoke in a dazed voice.

"Not . . . not Tory Brooke?"

"Yes."

"My dear, you *can't* be. It's quite impossible. Tory Brooke is a kind of distant cousin of mine, and she travelled from Portugal with a gentleman by the name of . . . Wait, I've got it written down in my diary. He was—"

"Mr. Darlan."

"That's right. He was to keep an eye on her and . . . Then you *are* Tory! You really are! Of course you must be, but I was looking for three people, not one—a child, that's you; a man, that's whoever you said just now—and a third person, a sister or something of that kind, who was to be picked up in Paris. Are you really Tory Brooke?"

"Yes."

"Then let me kiss you." The fur hood approached and brushed Tory's cheek. "Let me look at you. I can't believe it's you—you can't *imagine* how glad I am to see you. I daresay you know that I loved your father madly, once upon a time, and it's wonderful to meet his daughter. Is he still beautiful to look upon? I'm afraid to ask—time does such peculiar things to people, and you could see what it had done to me if you knew how I looked before. Why are we sitting on a cold bench on a freezing station when we might be at home, warm and comfortable? Let's go." She rose and led Tory towards the exit. "Would it be all right if once you'd got yourself rested and unpacked we went out to lunch? I don't cook anything at home if I can help it. Did your father tell you that I run a shop?"

"Yes."

"I got rather overexcited when I got his letter asking me to meet you and see you to school. All I'd had from him for about eleven years before that was a scrappy couple of lines written inside a Christmas card. I suppose he—" She halted, her forehead puckered. "I have a feeling I've forgotten something. Perhaps . . . Oh, your luggage. We can't walk off leaving your school trunk behind, can we?"

"It's at school."

"How did it get to school?"

"Mr. Paget drove it to England when he brought his daughters' luggage."

"Useful Mr. Paget. Is that suitcase all you've got?"

"Yes."

"Let me feel if it's heavy. Well, it's not light. Do you feel too weighed down to go home by bus instead of by taxi?"

"No."

"I don't own a car. I gave up driving when parking got impossible, long before Arabs were invented. There's a bus that stops at the end of my road, and if we sat on top, that's to say not on top but upstairs, you'd see some rather interesting bits of London, and as you've got so little time, why not make the most of it?"

"I'd like that very much. Thank you."

"But I've still got this feeling that I've forgotten something. Could it . . . Oh Tory, of *course!* Those people who brought you. We must go back—they'll think I'm frightfully rude to have carried you off without so much as a thank-you."

She turned, and had taken several steps before she realized that Tory was not beside her.

"You'd better come, too," she called, "unless you've already said good-bye to them. Even so, I ought to make a speech, but without you I won't have the faintest idea what they look like."

Tory went up to her and then stood still.

"They didn't come," she said.

"Who didn't?"

"Mr. Darlan and Madame Leblanc."

"Who's Madame Leblanc?"

"He said she was his sister, but she wasn't. She was waiting in Paris."

"What for?"

"For us—her brother, only he wasn't, and me. Mr. Darlan was travelling with me to England."

"Yes, Tory darling, I know. We established that. And now we must thank him. Your father wrote and said he was looking after you on the journey."

"He got off at Bayonne."

"He what?"

"He got off the train at Bayonne, and it went without him."

"But . . . you mean he just disembarked before the journey was half over, and left you?"

"He went after his luggage."

"Why should he go after his luggage at Bayonne?"

"He thought someone had taken it."

"Taken it where? I'm so sorry to appear dim-witted, but just *think* how confusing: your father says one thing and Mr. Darlan does another, and there's a Frenchwoman in Paris whom I haven't placed yet, except that she wasn't his sister, but if he's in Bayonne and she's in Paris, why are we looking wildly round to thank them for all the wonderful care they didn't take of you? I never"—she was once again leading the way to the exit—"I never in my life heard anything so extraordinary! They're supposed to be in charge of you—not that you look as though you need anybody to take charge of you, you're such a composed little thing—and where do I find you? On a bench, looking frozen and half-starved. Are you half-starved?"

"I'm hungry, yes."

"Then we'll stop at a milk bar on the way home. What did your father tell you about my shop?"

"He said you worked there part of the time."

"Mornings. I've been a partner for about eight years—I own a third share. The other two-thirds are owned by a brother and sister called Douglas and Fiona. They take over from me every day at one o'clock. It's called a china shop, but all we sell is plates and cups and things—dinner and breakfast and tea services, the special thing about them being that they're made from our own private design and people can always replace breakages, which means that they're never left with oddments. Here's where we wait for our bus. Just look at you, so neat and well-groomed—who'd believe you'd been in trains for the past two days? You get that from your father. He used to come back from far-flung places looking shaved and slicked and not a single piece of luggage lost, not at all like that impossible man who went chasing his luggage all over Bayonne. Did he send me any message?"

"Mr. Darlan?"

"Dear Tory, certainly not Mr. Darlan. I mean your father. He must have asked you to convey his compliments, if not his love. Here's our bus. Let's go upstairs and I'll show you the sights." She led the way up the stairs, adapting herself to the swaying of the bus like an experienced sailor. She made Tory take a seat by the window, and sat beside her.

"What were you saying? I know: you were giving me messages from your father. Do you know that I almost refused when he wrote and asked me to meet you? I don't know the first thing about children of any age, and I had no idea how I'd be able to entertain you. I didn't dream you'd be so . . . adult isn't the word I want, but you certainly don't have to be talked down to, so I can say what I like, which is such a relief. Your father rang up a few days ago to tell me that the children you were going to travel with had gone down with chicken pox and you were coming with I forget the name. If his letter sent me into a flutter, try and imagine what the sound of his voice did to me. How much did he tell you about me?"

Colour rose faintly in Tory's cheeks.

"Not very much," she admitted.

"He should have done. He must have done. He couldn't send you to me, a complete stranger, without filling in some background, surely?"

"Well, he . . . he isn't at home very much. He travels."

"I know he travels. All over the world, shut up in planes, a dull life, I'd say, but you surely get together when he gets home?"

"He isn't home for long."

"Long enough to catch up on his daughter's concerns. Don't tell me he's still the clam he used to be? I thought that marrying your mother would have changed him, brought him out, dragged him out of his shell. I never saw her, but I know people who did, and they said she was not only beautiful but vivid and—oh look, the Houses of Parliament. Too late. Does your father often talk about her?"

"No. Never."

"Never?"

"No."

"Do you have to learn about her from those old aunts and people?"

"They don't talk about her, either. At least, not much."

"You mean her name's never mentioned?"

"No."

"Good heavens above, why not?"

"Because . . . because of my father being so . . . so upset when she died."

"The word is shattered, Tory. And what man wouldn't have been? Married for less than eighteen months. My father thought it wasn't so much the accident and her death that shattered him but the fact that she wasn't used to driving in England and your father shouldn't have let her take the wheel of that great, powerful car, because of course when she had to react, she reacted on the wrong side of the road. But that was years and years ago, so I can't believe he's still shattered, and if he is someone ought to shake him into a sense of his paternal duty, and if I could get near him, I'd be the one. He—oh Tory, you missed the Guards, all so beautiful, and those heavenly horses, and all that scarlet. Never mind. Tell me about yourself."

They looked at one another—the quiet, ingrowing child and the calm, casual, easygoing, outgoing woman. Already one of the traits they had in common had been clearly demonstrated: their total lack of self-consciousness. Philippa had spoken, Tory had listened and answered questions as if they had been alone. They had not disregarded the people round them, they had simply been unconscious of their presence. They did not know, and if they had known would not have cared, that their conversation had been, was being followed with great interest by everybody within earshot. They had other similarities, the most notable of which was their ability to find a swift way round the obstacles that life placed in their paths.

"There's nothing to tell," Tory said at last.

"Your father's own daughter. Father clam and baby clam. Don't think for a moment that I'm advocating a ceaseless flow of chatter. I myself talk far too much. I know it, I deplore it—but will you just think what would happen if we were all like your father, only opening our mouths to communicate essentials such as that the house is on fire. *That* was the thing we used to argue about most: he thought I ought to say less and I thought he ought to say a good deal more. I wasn't surprised when I heard that your mother was a verbal fountain, like me; she had to be, to fill in the pauses. What's the use of cutting our beautiful human communication and merely grunting or wagging our tails to show what we're thinking? So you see that . . . Oh Tory, we shouldn't be talking. What did we come by bus for, and why did we come upstairs? To see London—and you've passed several interesting sights without so much as a glance. Now turn your face to the window and *gaze*. No, don't; we've got to get off. You go first, will you? Someone once slipped and came down right on top of me. I'll show you London some other time."

Tory had no desire to look at the sights. She wanted to go on looking at Philippa—looking and listening. She had forgotten the cold, forgotten her hunger, forgotten everything but the fact that in the course of a brief bus ride doors that had remained closed all her life had been pushed open, subjects that been avoided were freely discussed—freely and frankly. Never had she imagined that at her journey's end she would find anybody like this—unaffected but with a natural dignity, good-looking, gay. Within her was growing trust and a warm affection. For the first time in her life, she was surrendering to a person, a personality.

They got off the bus onto a busy street lined with shops and restaurants of the less expensive kind. After walking a short distance, Philippa stopped at a door above which was a sign:

ALPINE MILK BAR

MILK SHAKES. SANDWICHES

She led the way inside, and Tory, following her, found herself in a pastoral setting. The walls were decorated with Swiss mountain scenes, the tables were rustic, the predominating colours green and white. There were no tables; a counter in the shape of a horseshoe ran round the room, and behind it two women executed the customers' orders in unconcealed and reassuringly hygienic conditions. Philippa called a greeting.

"Morning, Milly. Morning, Clarice. I always come here," she explained to Tory as they settled themselves on stools. "I finish at the shop at one, and then I come in here and have hot soup and curry patties or cold soup and ham patties, depending on the season. And at all seasons, salads made as only Clarice can make them, with greenery and black olives and cheesy bits and raw shredded this and that. Clarice, this is my cousin Tory, who's staying a night with me before going off to school."

"Ah. The one you told me about." Clarice spoke with a strong Yorkshire accent. "My word, she's thin! Just come from Portugal, that's right, isn't it?"

"Yes," said Tory.

"Ah well, we'll fatten you up in no time, if you give us the chance," Clarice promised. "What'll it be this morning? Nice choco milk shake?"

"Yes, please."

"And how about a nice sandwich or two?" Clarice offered. "Choose what you like, but don't say peanut butter and jelly. Not peanut butter and jelly. All these kids round here ask for is peanut butter and jelly, and I'm sick to death of making 'em. But that's all they'll eat: peanut butter and jelly. I've got some lovely egg and cheese, or, if you'd rather, there's ham with shredded lettuce, or crabmeat, crab out o' the sea and not out of a can, with mayonnaise and—wait, I know what you'd really enjoy: minced chicken done my special way. Like to try that?"

"Yes, please."

"Yes, please," echoed Philippa, bringing Clarice's gaze to rest on her in surprise.

"You said I was to remind you to watch your weight, Miss Brackley. Is that watching your weight, chicken sandwiches at this time of the morning?"

"No, Clarice, it isn't, and you were right to remind me. Two for me, please, and two for Tory, and nice hot coffee for me, with a dab of cream. When we're through," she went on to Tory, as Clarice went to fill the order, "I'll take you along to the shop. It's only three doors away and I'd like to look in for a minute."

The shop, Tory found, was double-fronted, with both its windows displaying domestic china arranged in a series of intricate patterns.

"I do the window-dressing," Philippa said as they went in. She nodded to a woman who was attending to a customer in a far corner. "That's Fiona, but she's busy. Come and meet the other partner, Douglas."

Tory had met her father's partners and had found them uniformly bald and ageing, but affable. Douglas surprised her by being young and tall and lean and unfriendly to the point of hostility. He was sitting at a desk in a small, screened section of the shop. He rose when Philippa and Tory entered, picked up from the desk some pages that he had clipped together from a memorandum pad, and tossed them across to Philippa.

"If that's what you dropped in for," he said, "it's all there."

"I came in to thank you and Fiona for standing in for me this morning while I went to meet Tory."

His eyes were still on the papers.

"Seven phone calls in all," he said. "I told the business ones that you'd be back on the job tomorrow. I told the others—they were all male voices—that you'd call them back before lunch."

"Well, I won't. Not today. I'm going to keep today for Tory."

"Fortunate Tory. Would you mind very much if I got on with what I was doing when you dropped in?"

Philippa made no reply. Tory followed her into the cold, wet street.

"We can walk home from here, if you feel like it—it isn't far. Is your suitcase too heavy to carry?"

"No."

"Then let's walk and get warm. And don't take any notice of Douglas; he's upset. The partnership's breaking up."

"Why?"

"Fiona's decided to go back to her husband. She left him to join Douglas, and her husband went to a job in Canada. Now he's back, and they're going to get together again. Douglas doesn't think it'll work, but I do, and I'm glad she's going. And that means that I'm going, too. It worked as a threesome, but only because she knew how to manage her brother. I don't. To do him justice, he wasn't always the way you saw him just now; he's angry because things aren't working out the way he wanted them to. He was planning to expand the business. He can still expand, but it'll have to be with a new set of partners." She waited at a crossing, and led Tory across. "And now about you," she went on. "Tell me: How does your father get on with your great-aunts and your great-grandmother?"

"They don't live with us. I mean, it's the same house, but we have our own rooms and our own servants. My great-grandmother lives downstairs now because she's very old and she has to be near the chapel."

"Is the chapel, so to speak, on the premises?"

"It's part of the house, but it's got an entrance from the street. Once, people from outside used to come to Mass and they used that entrance, but now that the chapel's only used by the family the side gate's kept locked." She hurried on, the mention of the chapel having brought back for a moment the memory of Mr. Darlan. "My father and I live in our own part of the house."

"What happens when he goes on his travels?"

"Mademoiselle Barrault is with me."

"And who's she?"

"She used to teach French and music to my aunts."

"Then she can't exactly be bright young company, can she? Didn't your father ever consider building a nest of his own, with you and without Mademoiselle?"

"No."

"Then he should have done. I don't know how old your great-aunts are, but it can't be much fun for you, rattling round in a gigantic house with octogenarian aunts . . . Octo?"

"Sexa."

"I beg their pardon. Sexagenarian aunts. He should have given up all that world-ranging business and devoted more time to you, and I shall tell him so when I see him. Is he coming to meet you when you go back at Easter?"

"He said he might, but I don't think he will."

"Why not?"

"He won't come to England."

"He won't what?" Philippa paused on the point of crossing the road. "Why won't he?"

"Well, my aunts say it's because of what happened to my mother."

"Do you mean to tell me that not only is your mother's name never mentioned, but the fact that she died in a car accident in this country all those years ago means that your father will never visit it again?"

"Yes."

"Is that the real reason he didn't bring you over to England?"

Tory attempted what she felt to be a too-feeble defense.

"Well, he was going to Lima."

"But he hadn't already left?"

"No. He saw me off at the station."

"Kind of him. How very, very kind of him. Will you please take me safely across this road? I'm so angry, I'd probably walk into that bus or get mown down by a car. Don't think," she said when they had reached the other side, "don't think for a moment that I'm being disloyal to your father. We were practically brought up together—I suppose that's one of the things he hasn't found time to mention. His parents died when he was fifteen, and after that he spent all his school holidays with my parents. When he was up at Oxford, he spent all the vacations with us. I was eight years younger than he was, and I didn't really notice him at first, but once I did, I went on noticing. He . . . This is our road. My house is the end one, on the corner."

It looked to Tory very small. The road was wide and tree-lined; along one side stood a row of houses, all of the same design, each facing a small patch of front yard. On the other side of the road was a tall, wrought-iron gate through which could be seen extensive grounds and, through the trees, a large house. A plaque beside the gate stated that this was a boys' school. The line reading *for the sons of gentlemen* had been erased and *boys from 8 to 12* substituted. From the wild sounds coming from beyond the trees, it could be surmised that the boys were at play.

"The noise is intermittent," Philippa remarked. "Otherwise it's a nice, quiet road, and not a car-owner in it from end to end. Like myself, they discovered that it was quicker to walk."

She had stopped at the front door of number fourteen. She opened it and ushered Tory into a square hall floored in black and white tiles.

"Oh, nice and warm!" Tory exclaimed gratefully.

"Yes. The heating works beautifully, thank God. Take off your coat and hang it up and I'll take you on a swift tour." She hung her coat beside Tory's, took off her fur hood and shook out thick, softly waving hair. "First in here. Sitting room. Come and look."

What Tory came and looked at seemed to her merely an extension of the novelty that Philippa had been injecting into life since her arrival. It was an unexpectedly large room. The walls were tangerine, the wall-to-wall carpet a paler shade of the same colour. The woodwork was white, the upholstery black, the cushions tangerine and white. The sofa and four chairs were all of soft leather, shapeless, waiting to accommodate themselves to the forms of those who sat in them. The lights, low-slung, looked like halves of gigantic oranges. The small tables beside each chair and on each side of the sofa had black spongeable surfaces.

"People tell me," Philippa said, "that it looks like the VIP lounge of a space airport, or perhaps I should say a spaceport. Maybe it does, but when I was selling the house in Yorkshire after my father died, I said to myself: There goes the antique; now for the contemporary. When I bought this house, I found I didn't care for those jigsaw bits you can assemble to make anything from a bar to a bookshelf. I wanted colour—lots of colour. As you see, I got it. Now come and look at what should have been the dining room but had to be used as a library."

The room on the other side of the hall was small; its walls were covered by bookshelves, and the shelves were filled with books, some with beautiful bindings, some with their paper jackets still on them, others old and new paperbacks.

"I tried distributing the books round the other rooms, but there were too many of them," Philippa explained. "I can throw away most things—I'm no hoarder—but unless I really loathe a book, I have to keep it. So here they all are—some of my father's and the rest mine, right from the time I began to read. Come in whenever you like and make yourself at home. You'll find lots of variety: everything from *Black Beauty* to *Decline and Fall*. And now come and see the kitchen, which is rather nice, as that's where I eat and where my visitors eat, too." She opened a door. "Like it?"

Tory, taking in the white-and-primrose picture, found only one word to say.

"Yes."

"It's pretty, isn't it? I had to have a nice big table; I don't often cook, but when I do I need space to spread myself out, or to spread my pastry out. Come upstairs and I'll show you your bedroom."

They went upstairs, and Philippa opened two of the doors on the landing.

"Here you are: guest room. I'm next door. As you see, I've got the biggest window and the front view. The third room I use for junk. You overlook what I persist in calling a garden, but—"

She paused. Tory was still standing at the door of the larger room, looking in surprise at the photograph on the dressing table.

"My father," she said.

"That's right. Your father." Philippa went into the room and picked up the framed likeness. "This was taken up in Yorkshire, just after we got engaged. It doesn't really do him justice, but he . . . What's the matter?"

"Engaged!"

Philippa studied her for a few moments.

"Didn't he even mention that fact?" she asked.

"No."

"Well, I suppose I shouldn't be too surprised. I slipped out of his mind more than eleven years ago, when he went on one of his business trips to Macau and met your mother. But I don't see why he couldn't have told you that he was once engaged to me. He knows I never had any hard feelings about what happened. Why send you here without telling you how fond of him I once was? Why keep the memory of your mother wrapped in black crepe and put away?" She walked into Tory's room and sat on the bed. "I mustn't get worked up, Tory, over something that's over and done with—but I do feel that at the age of ten an intelligent child like you ought to be told a few family facts, even if they're scandalous, which these certainly aren't, unless you call being jilted scandalous, and I suppose that's what your father did to me, though, as I've just told you, I never held it against him—witness the fact that I keep his photograph on my dressing table, together with the little koala bear he won at some village fair or other on the day we got engaged. Why does he put up a shutter between you and the past? What possible reason can there be for his not saying to you: 'You're going to meet this cousin, no beauty but stacked with sense, to whom I was once engaged, but just before we were going to be married I had to go to Macau and there I met and fell madly in love with your beautiful mother.' How can any child grope its way through life if its parents or guardians tear up all the pages of the past? Nobody was more sorry than myself when your mother died, because from what I knew of her—it wasn't much, because they were so far outside my orbit—I gathered that she was gay and full of life and I thought that was just what was needed to make your father human. I don't want to say a word against him, but human he certainly is not. Even when I loved him, I could see how pretty awful he was in many ways, so I suppose it was a good thing our marriage never came off. If you're worrying about my state of mind subsequent to my being jilted, I ought to tell you that I got over it in due course, and got engaged to someone else. That one jilted me, too, but he didn't go all the way to Macau; he did it right here in England."

Tory took in air.

"Who?" she breathed.

"Oh, a man. He gave me up, or threw me over, or cast me off because I couldn't see any way out of going back to Yorkshire to look after my father, who'd had a stroke. There he was—my father, I'm talking about—alone in our house, which was a converted parsonage on the edge of some dreary moors, just like those unfortunate Brontë sisters, and when he got ill there was nobody to look after him—my mother was dead. So he sent for me. I tried to get somebody to take charge of him—a nurse, male or female, anybody—but he had only lost the use of one of his legs, not his mind or his tongue, and he made life hell for anybody I found—and no nursing home would keep him. So I couldn't see how I could get out of going, but this man—the man I was engaged to—took the view that I was being morally blackmailed by a selfish old man who must be made to see reason. And of course he was right about the selfish part, but I could remember a time, and so would your father, when my father was nice and kind and great fun to live with. That was before he got old and ill and bad-tempered. So I left London and that was the end of my engagement, and my father knew he'd broken it up, but all he was interested in was the fact that I was up there taking care of him. He'd forgotten how bad I was at anything domestic, especially cooking, and I shall never know why he didn't die in the first weeks of my ministrations. He almost did, but he rallied and set about making life hell until I'd learned to cook things the way he liked them. Which turned me into a first-class chef but left me, when he died, with a fixed determination never to cook anything again unless I had to. I sold the house in Yorkshire and came back to London and bought this one, and went into the china business, and that brings my life history up to date. Except to add that it's nice to have you here, and I'm glad you came." She rose.

"And now I'm going downstairs. Come when you want to, or stay up here, or if you didn't sleep on the train have a sleep now, or do anything you like."

Tory, left alone, did not take long to decide what she wanted to do. Stay up here? No. Sleep? Certainly not. She would unpack and then she would go down and continue listening to Philippa.

She opened her suitcase and took out her night things. She unwrapped the statuette, handling it carefully, and then re-wrapped it in the woollen garment. She would have to decide what to do with Saint Christopher—but not yet.

She went downstairs. Philippa was in the living room, tearing open the envelopes of the letters that had come by the morning mail. She led Tory into the kitchen.

"Sometimes I feel the house is too small," she said. "Its great drawback is that it doesn't stretch to visitors, except a small one like you. The outlook at the back—you can see it from this window —isn't what you could call picturesque. In fact, it's a dump."

Tory could see, beyond the low wall at the end of the garden, a piece of waste ground several acres in extent. Along one end ran the row of houses which included Philippa's. On the far side were houses of a different type, tall, handsome, standing in spacious grounds. On the other two sides of the area were roads—one the quiet, little-used one that ran past the side of Philippa's house, the other the main shopping district.

"The vacant space was going to be used for blocks of apart-ments," Philippa explained, "but there was an objection and they decided to make it a parking lot. Then they said no, it's to be Council houses. They're still arguing, and in the meantime it's become a recreation ground for the neighbourhood. As you see, there's a soccer field and there's a kind of arena which the pony club uses, and people exercise their dogs and the local schools use it as an extra playground, but fortunately there isn't a single tree on it to give shade, so we don't get any picnic parties leaving litter. We get a different kind of litter—rubbish-dump litter. Bicycle tires, car tires, any old iron. The boys from the school, and any other children who feel disposed, amuse themselves by hurling choice items over the back walls of this row of houses. The woman next door, who's an old horror by the name of Mrs. Dexter, had her wall built higher, too high for the things to come over it. I wait until it's dark and then I usually go out and throw the things back onto the dump. But you didn't come here to talk about rubbish dumps. You've only got one day, so let's make the most of it. I ought to take you to something instructive like the National Gallery or one of the museums, but how about going out to lunch and then seeing a show? You can often get tickets at the last moment. Shall we try?"

They tried, and succeeded in getting two seats for a ballet performance. When it was over, they decided against eating near the theater, and took a bus back to the milk bar. Then they walked through the dark, cold, slippery streets to the little, warm house. They watched television for a time and then went up to bed carrying cups of hot cocoa. The day was over.

Over. Tory put her cup on the dressing table, sat on the bed and faced the future. School, and then another day like this at the end of term before she went home for the holidays. Home. Not her home, not her father's home, not even her mother's home; the house that belonged to her great-grandmother. There seemed to her a serious lack in a language that labelled two such ludicrously differing establishments by the same name: home—the vast, marble-floored, cold, empty, echoing apartments of the Casa Fenix, or this warm, comfortable little box, three rooms upstairs and three rooms downstairs. Old ladies, forbidden topics, priests and prayers—or Philippa and free, very free speech. Where and what was home?

She got up and took the statuette out of the suitcase. Show it to Philippa, tell Philippa what had happened on the journey? She couldn't decide. She needed time to think . . . but there was no time. Tomorrow she would have to go. By tomorrow, she would have to show Saint Christopher to Philippa, or find a place in which to hide him.

Time. She needed time to think. Wasn't there something, anything she could do to delay her departure? All she needed was time to think, to plan, to decide. To think . . .

She closed her eyes. After a time, she opened them and walked slowly to the door of the bathroom. She went in, closed the door and stood leaning against it. There was one way . . . but wasn't it a risk? If Philippa had sharp eyes . . . But risk or not, it was the only possible hope.

Her decision made, she went back to her bedroom and undressed. Then she took from her suitcase her travelling writing pad. If only she had her crayons with her! If only the pen had red ink! But if she didn't press too hard it would be all right. It would be better to do it in the bathroom; do it, but not overdo it.

When she returned to her room, she remembered her cup of cocoa. It had become cold; she left it and climbed into bed. She had put out the ceiling light; by the dim glow from the bedside lamp she lay waiting. She did not have to wait long; Philippa had said that she would come and see her safely into bed, and here she was. She was wearing a blue dressing gown and her hair was drawn back with a green ribbon. She paused in the doorway.

"All ready for a nice sleep?" she inquired.

"Yes. Thank you for my nice day."

"You don't have to thank me, you have to thank God. Said your prayers?"

"Not yet."

"Oh, your drink!" Philippa advanced into the room. "You let it get cold."

"I didn't want it. I . . . I don't feel like having it."

Something in her voice made Philippa turn and look at her. She sat on the bed and took one of Tory's hands.

"Feeling homesick?"

"Oh no!" The instant denial carried conviction. "It's just that I think I've got—"

She paused, and Philippa looked puzzled.

"Got what, Tory?" she asked.

Tory opened the three buttons at the front of her nightgown and cautiously exposed a small area of chest.

"Spots," she said.

There was silence, broken only by Philippa's exclamation of dismay. Tory, without risking a closer examination, fastened the buttons and waited. Philippa spoke at last.

"Oh Tory, poor Tory! You've caught . . . What was it those girls had who couldn't travel with you?"

"Chicken pox."

"You've never had it?"

"No."

"Then that's what it is. How do you feel?"

"All right, I think. I haven't got a temperature."

Philippa's hand went out to feel her forehead.

"No, you haven't. But I'd better ring the doctor. I don't suppose he'll dream of coming out tonight, but I can ask him to come first thing in the morning. Do you think you'll get any sleep?"

"Yes, I think so."

"I'll bring you an aspirin and leave it by your bed, and if you can't drop off, take it." Philippa went to the medicine cupboard in the bathroom and returned. "I'm going to leave your door open, Tory. If you need me, all you have to do is call. Will you be sure to do that?"

"Yes. Thank you. Have you got the telephone number of the school?"

"The . . . Oh heavens, the school! Of *course*, the school must be told. No, I haven't the number—have you?

Tory, reaching over to the dressing table, produced from the writing case the school's telephone number.

"I'll phone them now," Philippa said. "What a good thing you remembered! They wouldn't have been at all pleased if you'd been missing from the school train tomorrow, and not a word about why. When did you realize you had spots?"

"A little while ago."

"Did you feel ill?"

"No."

"Just think of the trail of infection we've been leaving everywhere—train, station, milk bar, theater and so on. Half London

75

will break out in chicken-pox spots in a week or so. Lie down, Tory, while I phone. I'll have to send a telegram to your father, if we can locate him, to tell him you've been stricken."

"I've got a list of the places he's going to be in—he gave it to me so's I'd know where to write."

"Let me have it. And now, what's the number of the school? Did your father remember to tell you that I went there?"

"Yes. That's why he's sending me."

"It's not a bad place, as schools go. The grounds are wooded, and convenient for getting lost in. There was a nice headmistress in my day, but she's probably retired."

She telephoned from her bedroom, and her words floated out to Tory through the open doors.

Then she put down the receiver the went back to Tory's room. "A so-called secretary," she reported, "anxious to put over the idea that she's running the place single-handed. Do your spots tickle?"

"No."

"Mine did. If you feel well enough, ponder on how nice it's going to be for me to have you a little longer. We can—"

She stopped, went to the bed and very gently drew up the blankets. Tory, her purpose accomplished, had fallen asleep.

Chapter Four

She was awake early, and with waking came remembrance and the need for caution. In the bathroom, she sponged off the spots; then she went back to bed and was dozing when Philippa, pajama-clad, looked in. She opened her eyes and sat up.

"Good morning," Philippa said. "How do you feel?"

"I feel fine, thank you. I felt all right last night, too, except for having spots. They aren't there any more."

"Gone?" Philippa came to sit on the bed. "Really gone? Show me." She inspected the square of chest exposed by Tory. "You're right—not a sign. Do you think you had them when you left Portugal, without knowing?"

"No. Only last night."

"Well, it's very odd. I've rung the doctor; we'll wait and see what he says."

The doctor, Scottish and sparing of speech, arrived early and was informed of the recent exposure to two cases of chicken pox, and of the appearance and disappearance of the spots. He merely nodded, and proceeded to make an examination of the patient. His comment to Philippa, made as he replaced the stethoscope in his bag, was terse.

"Ye've wasted m' time."

"I've what?"

"Wasted m' time. She's no' ill."

"But she had spots last night," Philippa protested. "I saw them. She was supposed to be going away to school today, and when I rang them, I was told she couldn't go until a doctor had given her what they called a clearance. You can't expect them to—"

"Did ye say she'd just come frae Portugal?"

"Aye. I mean yes."

"By train, you said?"

"Yes."

"Then she mebbe took something that disagreed wi' her. She's as healthy as I am."

He walked to the door, went downstairs and put on his coat in silence. Then he clamped his hat on his head and waited for Philippa to open the front door.

"I've got to have some sort of certificate to show the school, haven't I?" she asked him.

"I'll no' sign a certificate to say that a child has recovered frae an ailment she hasna' had. Good morning to ye."

Philippa went upstairs and reported this unsatisfactory outcome.

"In my day," she went on, "you could go back when the last of the scabs had disappeared. If you didn't get spots after being in contact with chicken pox, I think you were pronounced pure after two weeks. So shall we split the difference and keep you here for ten days?"

"Yes. I'm sorry I'm giving you all this trouble."

"Tory, if you say anything like that ever again, I'll open the front door and push you right out into the snow. I can't bear to think of your going off to school just as I've got to know you. But you've got to go, so we'll make it ten days, and then I'll take you back myself, and when they ask for the certificate I'll look very upset and tell them I've unfortunately come without it. If that's deceiving, let it be placed on the debit side of the doctor's account on the tablets of heaven. Do you really feel all right?"

"Yes, I do. I feel fine."

"Then I don't see why you shouldn't get up. How about clothes? You've only that small suitcase; will you have enough to last you until you get to school?"

"Yes."

"Then that's all right. Would you mind if I went to work this morning? I took the morning off yesterday to go and meet your train, but I'd like to be back on the job this morning. Douglas and Fiona and I have a sort of code about not disturbing the routine unless there's an emergency—meeting you came under that heading. Will you mind being alone every morning?"

"No, I won't at all."

"Do whatever you like, and cook yourself anything you want to for breakfast. I only take toast and coffee, but there's enough food in the kitchen to keep you from starving: bacon, eggs, cans of this and that, and pints of milk, just help yourself. Can you find your way to the milk bar for lunch?"

"Yes."

"Then come along at about one o'clock and we'll have lunch together."

When she left the house, Tory got up and dressed. The idea of being alone gave her a sense of adventure, marred only by some brief moments of apprehension that Mr. Darlan might appear. He must certainly have the address of this house; would he come? She dismissed the possibility; how could he show himself when he must know that his theft had been discovered? The probability of her having told the story to the police would be enough to keep him away.

She enjoyed the morning. She explored the kitchen, found utensils and food and made breakfast for herself. She cleared the table, washed the plates and went upstairs to tidy her room, wishing that Angelina were there to compliment her on her success in her new role of housewife. She remembered Philippa's instructions about emptying the garbage pail, and went outside to tip its contents into the trash can standing at the back door.

She had replaced the trash-can lid and was about to go indoors when a noise at the end of the garden made her turn. She saw that an old car tire had been thrown over the wall from the waste ground, and was rolling to a stop on a flower bed. As she watched, a bicycle tire sailed over the wall and joined it.

She went up to her bedroom to make a reconnaissance. From the window she had a clear view of the road to the left, the neighbour's garden to the right, and in front the waste ground stretching to the tall buildings in the distance. A few schoolboys were playing soccer, supervised by an athletic-looking young master. Close to the wall of Philippa's garden, three boys were standing. Two of them were Asians and looked about fourteen. The third was white and weedy and looked about her own age. As Tory watched, one of the bigger boys threw over the wall the knob of a brass bedstead and an old felt hat.

She went downstairs, put on her coat and went into the garden. Reaching the wall, she picked up a chair leg—the latest offering —and hurled it back onto the waste ground. Its arrival was followed, to her dismay, by anguished yelps from a dog and shouts of protest from its owner.

"Hey, you! Let my dog alone, will ya?"

She went round the side of the house to the gate, and into the road. She walked to the corner and then made her way to the waste ground, and saw that the two older boys had retreated and were disappearing into the distance; the third boy was standing beside a very small mongrel puppy. She halted a few yards away.

"I'm sorry I hurt your dog," she said.

"Oh, it was you, was it?" His voice was shrill with indignation. "He didn't do anything. I didn't do anything, either. It was those other boys. All I was doing was just watching 'em, that's all."

His eyes, small and angry, stared at her from a thin, freckled face. His nose, so small as to be negligible, was tipped scarlet by the wind. His blue jeans were mud-streaked.

"Well, I'm sorry," she said again. "I saw things being thrown, but I couldn't see your dog."

She went nearer and put out a hand towards the little animal. After making a test or two to find out whether she could be

80

regarded as a friend, he wagged his long, curly tail and pushed his nose into her hand.

"What's his name?" she asked.

"Leo."

Apart from the dog's desert-sand colour, Tory saw no kinship to the king of beasts. As though sensing her doubts, Leo shook an imaginary mane and did his best to look dangerous.

"How old is he?" she asked.

"Four months. His birthday's in September. If you like, you can play with him. I haven't got any boys to play with. I did have until the school over the road finished its holidays, but now they've gone back and there's nobody. Do you want to play or don't you?"

"Yes."

He took a muddy tennis ball from one of the pockets of his jacket, and threw it across to her. She missed it, it rolled away and Leo leapt after it. The game was played for the benefit of the dog, but in running to intercept the ball, dodging, throwing and attempting to catch, Tory grew warm. When Leo dropped to a crouching position on the wet ground, hung out his tongue and proceeded to pant, the boy called a halt. The ball, wet and slimy, was replaced in his pocket, and the three began to walk towards the road.

"What's your name?" Tory asked.

"Derek. What's yours?"

"Tory."

"Never heard that before." His eyes narrowed suspiciously. "I bet you're making it up."

"No. I'm not. It's short for Vitorina."

"You a foreigner or something?"

"Half."

"What're you doing in that house? There's somebody called Miss Brackley lives there."

"She's my cousin. I'm staying with her until I go to school."

"When's that?"

"In ten more days."

"Boarding school?"

"Yes. Where do you go to school?"

"Nowhere. I used to go to that school across the way, but my mother took me away because we're going to live in Eastbourne, so that's where I'll go to school."

"When will you go away from here?"

"What's today?"

"Wednesday."

"Then it's about six days more. My mum's gone already. She went with my stepfather. They're going to look for a house, and I'm staying with our landlady till I go. We're going by train, me and Leo. We're going from Victoria Station, by ourselves."

"Leo'll miss you when you go away to school."

"Who said I was going away to school? Catch me at a boarding school. I'm going to a day school."

"Where does your landlady live?"

He waved a hand in the direction of the tall houses on the other side of the waste ground.

"Over there. Colony Street."

"Do you always bring Leo onto this waste ground to exercise him?"

"Where else is there? He's no good on roads. When we're on a road, I have to keep him on a leash."

"Do you come every day?"

"Have to. He brings his leash and kicks up a barking noise until I bring him. Some days I can't stay long, because I have to go and buy something to eat, because if I didn't, I wouldn't get anything. My landlady's supposed to cook, but she doesn't; she's too fat and lazy. All she does is hand over the dough and then I buy what I like, fish 'n chips, mostly. It was like that when my mum was here; if my mum didn't cook something, we didn't get it. Where're you going to go now?"

"Back to the house."

"She's not there, is she? Miss Brackley, I mean. Mrs. T. says she goes out to work."

"Mrs. T.?"

"The landlady. She knows all about everybody round here. You can come and see her if you like."

"She hasn't asked me."

"You kidding? That's all she likes doing, talking to people. She's got bad legs, so she doesn't go out much, but she could stand on 'em long enough to cook, if she wanted to. She says she was an actress once, but my mum said she made it up. Coming?"

Tory hesitated for a few moments. A glance at her watch told her that it was not yet eleven o'clock; whether she walked to the milk bar or went by bus, there was a good deal of time to spare. She nodded, and turned with Derek in the direction of Colony Street.

The backs of the houses looked badly in need of paint, but apart from this, a real-estate agent, viewing the buildings from Philippa's house, would have been justified in describing them as desirable. Tory imagined Colony Street to be a wider version of the quiet, tree-lined Elcombe Grove, so she was surprised as she approached it to note a constant stream of cars going to and from the main shopping center. Turning the corner, she discovered that Colony Street was no quiet thoroughfare, and the houses no longer desirable. All of them, on both sides of the road, showed clear signs of cheap, makeshift division and subdivision. Clothes hung on lines that had been slung between windows; tenants, brown or black or white, were to be seen going in and out of doorways. There were no front yards; once-handsome, scarred stone steps led up to the main entrances, and on the top step were perambulators, their wheels wedged by bricks or wooden blocks. Children played on the pavements, along which an unending succession of cars was parked, white lines indicating the spaces not to be trespassed upon. As well as the white lines, there were scrawled warnings: *This for Joe Memba's car* or *Don't you park here, this for Susy's Mini.* The noise of traffic, of yelling children, mingled with the sounds of social interchange as neighbour shouted to neighbour. Tory, her heart lifting, felt that she was walking through one of the streets of the Alfama district in Lisbon; these houses were larger, the street wider, but here, as there, family life spilled out of doors.

Derek was walking down iron steps that led to a semi-basement.

Tory followed him. The yard at the bottom appeared to be the repository for all the rubbish of the house—there were seven trash cans, most of them overfull. He opened a door, ushered Tory into a dark passage and switched on a light.

"Mrs. T.! Brought a visitor," he shouted.

Tory saw three doors, all open. On view were a small, dirty, littered kitchen and a lavatory no bigger than a cupboard. The third room was a bedroom—like the kitchen, littered, the bed unmade. Derek was opening a fourth door and pushing aside a heavy, soiled curtain that hung in the doorway. A wheezy voice was heard behind it.

"Hello, Derek, ducks."

Tory followed him into a room so full of furniture that it was difficult to locate where the voice had come from. Then she saw, seated in one of the four battered armchairs ranged round a gas heater, a woman of massive proportions dressed in what looked like a flannel nightgown. Two small, faded blue eyes peered at Tory from beneath an auburn wig that had slipped sideways. The swollen hands held knitting, the needles as thick as pens, the wool eight-ply.

"Come in, ducks. Come in and sit down. Derek'll take them things off if you wait a minute. That's right; take a seat."

Tory sat down. On every part of the walls not obscured by furniture were pasted unframed photographs or snapshots. Piles of newspapers lay on every available surface; china ornaments on which were painted the arms of English cities had been placed on cupboard tops, plastic feathers waved from plastic ducks above the fireplace.

The shrewd little eyes were on Tory, but the hands were going on with their task of knitting.

"Where did you say you met Derek, dearie?"

"On the waste ground," Derek told her. "She threw a bit of wood at Leo. Over the wall."

"Which wall? Not . . . "

"No, not that one. I told you, but you never listen. Mrs. Dexter's gone and had her wall built a lot higher, so you can't throw things over it even if you want to. Not unless you get a ladder."

"Introduce me to your little friend," his landlady requested.

"She lives in Portugal."

"That's not an introduction. Where's your manners? I'm Mrs. Tesworth, dearie. What's your name?"

"Tory, that's what her name is," Derek informed her. "It's short for . . . short for what?"

"Vitorina," Tory said.

"Didn't you have any other names they could've called you?" he asked. "Or is that all of it?"

"No. There's more. Vitorina Piedade Jesuina Azevedo Brooke."

There was a pause.

"Jesus Superstar!" exclaimed Derek in stupefaction.

"You let me catch you sayin' anythin' like that again," Mrs. Tesworth told him fiercely, "an' I'll write straight off to your mum. You've picked it up from those—"

"Hey, cut it out," he broke in. "You're showing off again."

"I am doin' nothin' of the kind."

"Yes, you are. You're trying to talk posh, like when you talk to Mr. Barlow."

"I am mindin' my diction. Any objection to that?"

"Yeah. It's putting it on, that's why. It's pretending."

"Oh, you think so, do you? When your mum brought 'er friends in 'ere, what did she tell you to go and do?"

"Get the hell out."

"No, she did not. She told you to go and clean yourself up. She told you to show your 'air a comb for a change. She told you to take the mud out of your nails. So when you bring in company, I offer the same cortessy, that's all."

"What's cortessy?"

"It's what those people 'ad to 'ave in olden days, people who used to 'ang round kings and queens. It means bowin' and mindin' your manners, because if they didn't, they were chucked out. That was the first speakin' part your grandfather 'ad, and splendid 'e looked in 'is corteer tights. And 'e knew 'ow to bow, too." Mrs. Tesworth, embarked on her favourite topic, was paying less and less heed to diction. "Off with 'is 'at, such a flourish as you never saw, and one leg stretched out—like this." She dropped her knitting in order to illustrate, one hand on her vast stomach, the other holding aloft an imaginary hat. Grotesque as she looked, Tory, watching, saw clearly the image of a gentleman making a courtly bow. Her distaste for the room, for the surroundings, for Mrs. Tesworth, began to fade; she had caught her first faint glimpse of a picturesque past, of a Mrs. Tesworth who was to emerge from this mountain of flesh and become more real in fable than in fact.

"Did Derek tell you 'is father was an actor?" she asked Tory.

"No, I didn't," Derek answered. "She doesn't care what he was. What's it matter what he was?"

"It matters a lot," Mrs. Tesworth told him. " 'E was a good actor. So was your granddad. Your granddad would've done well if 'e'd stuck to costume parts. 'E looked a treat dressed up in short coats and fancy pants, like Sir Walter Raleigh, only 'e wanted big parts, and when 'e did get 'em, once or twice, 'e wouldn't bother to learn 'is lines. Your dad was different; 'e was a born comic, but like a lot of born comics 'e wanted to be 'amlet. If 'e'd stuck to being a comic, I bet you would've seen 'is name in lights now, instead of on a gravestone, if they gave 'im a gravestone, in some Gawd-forsaken Australian cemetery. 'E died in Australia," she explained to Tory. "Went there to make 'is fortune, an' met 'is death. That was two years ago, and that's when Derek's mum came to live with me, because I'd known 'er since before she was born, as you might say, an' she wanted to be near someone who'd known 'im and could talk about 'im to Derek. Only Derek never wanted to hear nothin' about what was gone. I didn't want any lodgers. There's not enough room 'ere for extras, and I told 'er so, but she said I wouldn't 'ave to do anythin', she'd do all the work, and so she did for the first week, and after that she went and got 'erself a job in a 'airdresser's. She said it was because she wanted to get money to pay to send Derek to that school round the corner in Elcombe Grove, but—"

"That's where Tory's living," Derek broke in. "Number fourteen."

"Number fourteen? That's Miss Brackley's house. You a friend of 'ers?" Mrs. Tesworth asked Tory.

"She's my father's cousin. I'm staying with her until I go to school—in about ten days."

"Boarding school, I expect, if you live in Portugal. I wanted to go to Portugal, once upon a time, but they didn't run package tours in them days. Only place I've seen outside England is Spain, and I did a package tour there with an old pal of mine, name of Mr. Barlow, because 'e'd played one of the soldiers in *Carmen* once, and got an idea 'e'd like to take a look at them fancy 'ats. Funny thing to want to do, after more than forty years, I said to him. Your cousin, Miss Brackley, she bought that 'ouse she's in, didn't she?"

"Yes."

"Thought so. I bet that's gone up in value, too, but living next door to Mrs. Dexter, like she does, that'd put people off buying, if she wanted to sell. I mean people from round 'ere, who know Mrs. Dexter. I've said time and time again that Miss Brackley's crazy to take as much as she does from 'er. 'As she told you what that old witch gets up to?"

"No."

Derek stood up and moved to the door.

"Anything to eat?" he inquired.

"Not till you go out and buy it. Here, gimme my purse off that table and I'll give you the money and you can pop round and buy yourself somethin', and you can get me a couple of slices of 'am, and a loaf and six eggs, and go down to the paper shop and tell 'em the telly programs didn't come again this week."

"You said you were going to cook a meat pie."

"I didn't get 'round to it. I 'ad to finish doin' the pools. Oh, a letter came from your mum; I put it on your bed."

He made no move to get it. He was putting on his coat. Leo had left his place beside the fire and was at the door.

"Coming?" Derek asked Tory.

"No, leave 'er 'ere," Mrs. Tesworth said. "She can talk to me till you get back." When the door closed, she unrolled the length of knitting and held it up for inspection. "I knit a lot of the time," she said. "I can knit and look at the telly, too. It's only plain 'an purl. Scarves is all I do; I sell 'em to the people up and down this street; not the young 'uns, oh no, not them, they're too dressed up to be seen dead in a thing like this. They buy 'em for their mums and dads and the old people, poor devils who didn't know what they was coming to when they came to this climate. And babies, too; they wrap the babies in 'em and keep them warm, so—" She broke off as a knock came at the door. "Who is it?"

The door opened, the curtain was pulled aside and the face of an old man appeared.

"Oh, it's you. Come on in and see Derek's friend," Mrs. Tesworth invited. "Here's Mr. Barlow what I was telling you about, Tory, ducks. Ernie's his name, but he called himself Maurice in his singing days. Take a seat, Ernie."

There had been no change in her manner, but her accent had undergone a noticeable improvement. Mr. Barlow was tall and thin, with a small, shrunken face and straggling white hair. He spoke in a soft, slightly husky voice, in which very little trace of Cockney could be heard.

"I met Derek," he said, "and he told me he'd brought a little girl from Portugal to see you. So I came to see her."

"Name of Tory, and lives with her cousin Miss Brackley, next door to you know who," Mrs. Tesworth said.

"Oh dear, oh dear." He turned worried eyes on Tory. "No trouble there lately, I hope?"

"Tory doesn't know anything about it yet, so maybe I shouldn't say this to her, but all I will say, Tory, ducks, is that that Mrs. Dexter is a whole snakeful of poison, and if Miss Brackley ever hears any tales about me, you can tell her where they came from. I don't know why Mrs. Dexter's always 'ad it in for me, but got it in for me she 'as, and—"

"And you know quite well why," Mr. Barlow put in in his quiet voice. "You know very well."

"She came 'ere complaining that Derek 'ad thrown things over her wall. I asked her 'ow she'd managed to pick him out of all the other boys who threw things, an' we got to words and she used some she'd picked up in a bar, and I picked up my 'andbag that was laid on the table, and I swung it and caught her one on the side of the 'ead."

"Which was a mistake," said Mr. Barlow, "because now Mrs. Dexter has got it in for Derek, too."

"Well, she can't hurt 'im. He 'asn't got long now," Mrs. Tesworth said. "Just so long as 'e keeps 'is dog out of 'er garden, 'e'll be all right." She sat lost in meditation for a few moments. "Wonder 'ow 'e'll get on with his new stepdad."

"He likes him," Mr. Barlow said in surprise. "Why shouldn't he get on with him?"

"He only knew him as a master at that school. That's very different from 'aving 'im as a stepdad."

"What did he teach?" Tory asked.

"Music," Mrs. Tesworth told her. "Derek wasn't interested, and none of the other boys was, much, but this chap kept on trying to find some geniuses, because he was keen on getting up an orchestra. Derek felt sorry for 'im and offered to learn the fiddle, if 'e could get 'old of a fiddle to learn on."

"Does he play now?" Tory asked.

"Not now, and not then, neither. 'E made his mum go and see this chap, to talk about a violin, and when those two met they forgot about the orchestra. They forgot about Derek, too, so Mr. Barlow went out and bought 'im a puppy, and the difference it made to that boy, I can't tell you. Isn't that right, Ernie?"

"Quite right."

"If anything happened to Leo, I don't know what 'e'd do, and that's the truth. But it'll be all right; they'll never 'ave the money to send 'im to a boarding school, so 'e'll have Leo every day. I gave 'is mum a straight talk before she went off; I told 'er that dog was more than company for Derek, it was the only company Derek 'ad. She saw what I meant."

"He'll need a dog ticket for the train," Mr. Barlow reminded her.

" 'E's got one. Got 'is own, too. 'E went down yesterday evening and bought 'em both with the money 'is mum left."

"Are you going to see him off?"

"Me? Put 'im on a train and watch 'im go? No. You can go if you like."

"If you're not going, I'll come along here and keep you company."

"That's right. Dry me tears. I wish 'e'd never come 'ere. You don't miss what you've never 'ad, but I've had 'im around for nearly two years, and honest to Gawd, I don't know what I'll do without 'im."

"You'll do what you've always done—put a good face on it," Mr. Barlow told her.

"That's right, I will. We went through some hard times, didn't we, Ernie?

"We went through some good times, too."

"Yes, we did. And for all that people 'ave nowadays, I can't see they're any 'appier than we were. All I ever 'ear is grumbling. 'Ere's Derek. Why don't you stay and have a bit to eat, Tory?"

Tory rose.

"I've got to go, thank you very much," she said. "I've got to meet my cousin at one o'clock."

"Then come again," Mrs. Tesworth invited. "It was nice seein' you."

Derek came in, dropped the review of television programs on the table and went into the kitchen to put away the eggs and the bread and to unwrap the fish and chips he had bought. Mr. Barlow rose, helped Tory on with her coat and opened the door for her.

She walked to the milk bar. It was cold, but she went slowly, lingering to look at the shop windows along the way, but with her mind elsewhere. Interesting as she had found Mrs. Tesworth, she realized that while she had been listening to the wheezy voice a subconscious balancing of accounts had taken place. She had worked out her problem. She knew what she was going to do about Saint Christopher.

She found Philippa waiting for her, seated at the counter of the milk bar and reserving the seat next to her.

"You've got nice pink cheeks," she said. "Did you walk?"

"Yes, but I was out on the waste ground, too."

"Exercising?"

"Playing with a dog. I threw something at it by mistake. When I went outside to empty the garbage pail, I saw things being thrown over the wall, so I began to throw things back."

"Goodness! Doesn't that come under the heading of provocation?"

"I don't know. I hit a dog by mistake. It's called Leo."

"Large and fierce?"

"No. Small and friendly. I heard it yelp, so I went round to the waste ground and I met the boy it belongs to. His name's Derek."

"Derek . . . Wan and weedy, with marmalade-coloured hair?"

"Yes. He knew you lived in the house I'd come from, but he didn't say he knew you."

"He doesn't. I know him because he's one of the topics of conversation at the local shops, and I hear snippets when I do my weekend shopping. Such as what a shame it is that his mother's married again and gone to live at Eastbourne."

"Why is it a pity?"

"Nobody's ever explained, but there seems to be a difference of opinion as to whether the music master was lucky to get her or whether she was lucky to get the music master."

"Where's Eastbourne?"

"South coast. What's known as a resort. Hotels and hydros. And schools—good, clean air, lots ot it."

"I went to see his landlady."

"Whose landlady?"

"Derek's. Her name's Mrs. Tesworth. Do you know snippets about her?"

"Not one. Did you get a surprise when you saw Colony Street?"

"Yes."

"So did I. If I'd seen it before I'd bought the house, I might have hesitated, because when you get the kind of congestion they've got there it eventually spreads, and where could it spread but in the direction of Elcombe Grove? Go on about the landlady."

"She talked about Mrs. Dexter. You know, the one who—"

"—lives next door to me. Yes, I know. What did she say?"

"She's sorry for you, having to live next door to someone like that."

"I'm sorry, too. Venomous is the only word that describes her. She's got a grudge against all humanity. She used to go and make frequent reports to the police, but she overdid it, and they got tired of her—the old story of crying wolf. She's quarrelled with every shop in the district, butcher and baker and grocer and all the rest. Now she has to take a bus every morning to the next group of shops, and when she's antagonized them, which she soon will, she'll have to go further afield. If you think I'm being unkind, just you wait until the wind's in the west, and you'll see."

"See what?"

"The contribution she makes to neighbourly relations. She waits for the days on which the wind will carry things from her incinerator into my garden, and then she lights it and feeds it with anything that'll rise and waft itself over the hedge onto my flower beds. Paper, mostly."

"Can't you stop her?"

"No. I complained in fairly strong terms, but I was outclassed. The neighbours on the other side of her—the east-wind side—told her what they thought of her, and she took it down on tape and there was a court case, which came to nothing but which her neighbours had to pay for. So now I try to pretend she isn't there. Shouldn't we stop talking and order something to eat? When we get home, I'll write my letters and maybe you could find something to amuse you, and then you can get the tea ready."

Getting the tea ready took longer than Tory had anticipated, but at last the things were assembled and she carried the tray into the sitting room. Philippa was putting a letter into an envelope; she stamped it and spoke.

"To your father," she said. "I've told him what I think of him for sending you to England in the care of a man who abandoned you halfway through the journey without so much as a word of explanation."

"It was the luggage—"

"His luggage was a secondary consideration. His first duty was to see you safely to England. What's more, he told lies. He told you, or he told your father, that that woman, Madame Something, was his sister. I can't understand your father even knowing a man like that, let alone confiding you to his care. Who was he, a great friend?"

"No. He and my father played golf sometimes."

"Does this man live in Portugal?"

"Only in the winter."

"Did your aunts know him?"

"Not until he offered to look after me on the journey."

"He offered?"

Tory made no reply. She was absentmindedly turning the sugar spoon over and over in the sugar. Philippa watched her.

"Tory, is anything the matter?" she asked with a touch of anxiety.

Without answering, Tory went upstairs. When she came back to the sitting room, she was holding the statuette, hidden in the folds of the woollen garment in which she had wrapped it.

"What's that?" Philippa inquired. "It looks like a woollen undershirt."

Tory had laid it on one of the small tables and was unwinding the soft folds.

"Yes, it is," she said. "I used it to wrap up . . . this."

It was not a dramatic announcement; it was a quiet statement. The wrapping was off. The statuette stood on the low table. Philippa looked at it, opened her mouth to speak, but could say nothing. At last she gave a long-drawn-out sound of astonishment.

"Tory! What's . . . what's that?"

"Saint Christopher."

"But it looks . . . Surely it's gold? I mean, outside."

"All through." She picked up the statuette and held it out. "Feel the weight."

Philippa held it, the colour leaving her cheeks.

"Solid?" she breathed.

"Yes."

"But . . . but this is impossible. Tory, do say something to clear it up. You can't just walk downstairs with a solid gold statuette and . . . You must be wrong. It can't be solid gold. If it were, it would be worth . . . well, I don't know how much, but an awful lot."

"It is."

"Where did you get it?"

Tory told her. It was a brief account; then she waited in silence for Philippa's comments.

The first was the one she expected.

"But Tory, why on earth . . . I mean, why didn't you tell me all this as soon as you arrived? Why did you wait until now?"

"I didn't know you. After I found it, I thought I might be able to leave it in your house, somewhere in my room until I came back on my way home to Portugal."

"You thought you could hide it here?"

"There are houses where it could be hidden. The maids think my great-grandmother hid it."

"But if they thought that . . . how could they imagine that . . . " She broke off. "I don't understand."

"She's very old, and lately she's been hiding things and pretending they're lost. This time, she didn't say Saint Christopher had been lost; she said he'd been stolen. But nobody believed her."

"But when they fail to find the statuette—which they will, since it's here with us—surely they'll inform the police? And then—"

"No. Sometimes it's a long time before they find out what she's done with the things, and they pretend to stop looking, and then when Father Diogo comes to hear confession she tells him and he goes and gets the things and gives them to the maids."

"But think what this thing's worth! Nobody, not even your Portuguese relations, could let a treasure of this kind vanish for long without getting suspicious, without thinking it's been stolen."

"It couldn't have been stolen—that's what they'd think. It was in the chapel when Father Diogo said early Mass, and I don't see how it could have been stolen afterwards. Nobody could have got in from the street because there's a guard at that gate. He's called Guilhermo. The maids were working in Aunt Jesuina's rooms and in the corridors leading to the chapel, so they wouldn't believe it could be stolen. But I've got to tell them about finding it in the luggage, haven't I?"

"Of course."

"But it wouldn't be any use telling the Portuguese police, because Mr. Darlan isn't there."

"We don't know where Mr. Darlan is." Philippa put the saint back on the table and turned it slowly to examine it from every angle. "This is the first treasure I've ever handled," she said. "I've seen things of this kind at a distance, in churches, in museums—but close, like this, never. Why is it so beautiful, Tory, can you tell me that? All it is, when you break it down, is a fat monk holding a baby."

"That isn't a baby. It's the Infant Jesus."

"It's . . . Oh, I see. And He's having a ride on—"

"Saint Christopher took him across the river."

"The river Jordan?"

"I don't know. I only know that it was Saint Christopher who carried people across the river because there was no bridge."

"That's why they made him a saint?"

"I think so. Well, yes. One day he was carrying a child and it seemed awfully heavy and then he heard a voice telling him that it was the Infant Jesus."

"I see. I thought it was standing in the niche in the chapel that had given it a religious aura. It's beautiful. It's more than beautiful;

95

it's got a kind of *glow*. I wish I thought that this Darlan had stolen it because he fell in love with it—but of course he took it because he could see what it was worth. And now I can understand a lot of things, such as why he didn't telephone to ask whether you'd arrived safely. I can also understand why Madame . . . what was her name?"

"Leblanc."

"I can understand what Madame Leblanc was waiting for. Not to come to England with you, but to let him pass the statuette to her." She frowned. "But there are other puzzling things. If this saint was in your basket, the basket you left at Austerlitz, what made Darlan get into a panic and chase after what he thought was his luggage? Surely there couldn't have been anything in his suitcases which was worth more than the statuette? If there had been, how was it that he was willing to open up for the French Customs? Did they look inside his golf bag?"

"No."

"Stuffed with loot, I'm willing to bet. And you've had this up in your room ever since you came, and not a word about it until now. Don't you think we ought to inform the police?"

"No."

"Think, Tory. There's a thief named Darlan walking round, free and unapprehended. Don't you want him to be caught?"

"Yes. But nobody will believe what I tell them about how I got Saint Christopher. If I said Mr. Darlan had taken it, and they asked him, he'd deny it, wouldn't he? He might even say that I'd taken it. My aunts would know that I hadn't, but how would the police know?"

"The job of the police is to find out. Here we sit, and in our possession is a stolen statuette worth a good deal of money. If we don't tell the police, we're stuck. We can't get it back to Lisbon, and we can hardly send a telegram to your aunts to say you've got it and will return with it at Easter. You'd have to offer some kind of explanation. The thought that Darlan and his accomplice, Madame Lesomething, are walking round free to go on stealing more statuettes makes my blood run cold. What other course do we have but calling in the police? I hate the thought as much as you do, but—"

"They'd ask questions, and they wouldn't believe the answers. It might be put in the papers, and they'd see it at school and . . . Oh Philippa, do we have to?"

Philippa studied her in silence. The last words had been spoken not on a high note of panic, but in a low, stifled voice that contained a desperate appeal. She ran over in her mind the events that would follow on a telephone call to the police. They would come and of course they would ask questions, and the answers were going to sound very weak. Tory's story of Mr. Darlan and his luggage, her basket, his shirt, Madame Leblanc . . . dragged out, laid out, probed and analyzed, how would it sound? And what effect would questioning and cross-questioning have on this child, who had already been through an experience that would have shaken anybody twice her age?

She sat lost in thought, and Tory watched her, afraid to break the silence, only her eyes showing the anxiety with which she awaited a decision. At last Philippa spoke.

"Tory—"

"Yes?"

"What you want, what I'd like to arrange if it's possible, is a way of dealing with this problem without calling in the police and without getting ourselves deep into a police inquiry and everything that a police inquiry would entail—right?"

"Yes. But—"

"Wait a minute. The first essential, as I see it, is to get word to your great-aunts and your great-grandmother that the statuette is safe. I include your great-grandmother because, from what you told me of seeing her that morning in the chapel, I've got a curious feeling that she knew something about how the thing was stolen."

"If she knew, she would have told me. She would—"

She stopped, her mind going back to her last meeting with Jesuina. Jesuina had been about to say something—but she had not said it. She had remained silent. Why?

"I think she was going to say something," she amended, "but she changed her mind."

"Which left everybody to suppose that she'd taken it herself, which they should have known she couldn't have done if she's as frail as you say she is. That thing weighs a lot; how could she have taken it down from its niche and staggered about looking for a place to hide it? She couldn't. Where are we? Oh, the police. You don't want to call them in, and I'm not anxious to, either. But we have to get the saint back to Portugal, yes?"

"If we can."

"And as law-abiding citizens we ought to find some way of seeing that the thieves are caught. Mr. Darlan is a thief, and it's pretty obvious that Madame Le . . . Leblanc belongs to the same racket. We therefore have to accomplish three miracles. One: We have to get the statuette back to Portugal. Two: We have to keep the police out of it. And three: We have to catch the culprits. Have I left out anything?"

"No. But—"

"But what?"

"How do we . . . I mean, we can't."

"You and I can't. But if we could get hold of someone who operated at the topmost level, someone who by waggling a finger could start all the lesser fry moving, someone who could give orders and see that nothing leaked out that we didn't want leaked—then we'd be in business, wouldn't we?"

"Yes. But—"

"Don't say 'but.' This whole thing is crawling with 'buts.' We need help, and we need help at the very highest level, and now comes the trouble: We need a Cabinet Minister, at the very least, and I don't know any Cabinet Ministers. Do you?"

"No."

"If my father had been alive, he could have helped. He was only a professor, but he was rather a special one, one of those international great brains, and people used to find their way across the lonely moors and sit at his feet; high-level personages, most of them. But when he died I lost touch with them all. Today, there's only one man I know, that's to say only one man with whom I'm acquainted, who moves in the highest circles, professional and social and political. But I'm not sure that he'd feel disposed to lend his weight to our problem."

"Who?"

"He used to be plain Tom Tancred, until they made him a life peer. Once upon a time, he and I were engaged to be married."

"Oh. The one who . . . ?"

"The same. We didn't part friends; he called me several names, of which pigheaded was the most polite. So will he feel disposed, now, to perform three miracles for us?"

"I don't know. Is he in London?"

"Yes. He's in an enormous office in the Haymarket and he has the ears of the high and mighty."

"Are you going to ask him? Will he . . . "

"Will he help us? Who knows? I'm going to find out. He can't say I've ever asked him to do anything for me before, and I'm not anxious to ask him to do something now, but we're in a desperate situation and it requires desperate remedies. I'm going to pay a friendly call on Lord Tancred, and with your permission I'll take Saint Christopher with me. Does this saint have any special powers, for instance carrying a life peer across the river of objections he's going to raise?"

"I suppose saints can do anything."

"Well, let's find out. I can't take him wrapped in an undershirt." She rose. "Let's find something more suitable, and a bag to carry him in." She paused to look again at the statuette. "How you could have slept soundly with this on your mind beats me. I wouldn't have been able to believe it if I hadn't happened to know your father so well. Don't, Tory, don't, *please* don't grow into a complete clam. I think discretion's right and necessary at times, but the power of communicating with your fellow creatures is also right and necessary. Would you mind if I asked Lord Tancred to keep Saint Christopher in his strongest safe until we can get him back to the chapel he was stolen from?"

"No, I wouldn't mind. I think it's a good idea. When will you go and see him?"

"Lord Tancred? Now."

"Now?"

"Now. I know he's in London, because it said so in yesterday's paper; he's presiding at some conference or other."

"Does my father know him?"

"Yes. They were up at Oxford together, but I wouldn't call them friends. They were in different lines of business, and your father was more away than at home, so they didn't often run across one another. They're quite opposite types. Lord Tancred got himself to the top the hard way; he's a fighter, which your father isn't. Now let's get Saint Christopher properly wrapped up, and then I'll go. He'll have had lunch, so he'll be in a mellower mood than he would be if I waited until tomorrow morning—and that would mean another morning off work, which I'd like to avoid if possible. Speaking of work, I worked for Lord Tancred once."

"As a secretary?"

"You could call it that. I certainly sat in front of a typewriter and peered at some incomprehensible squiggles I'd made in a notebook, and I tried to disentangle what he's said into machines, and I made the tea. It was my first job after leaving home the first time. And until the china shop, my last. What do you suggest we use for wrapping round Saint Christopher? I know—I've got the very thing: a silk scarf."

"Do I have to go with you?"

"No. Not this time. If he wants to see you, he'll say so."

Tory drew a long, relieved breath.

Chapter Five

Lord Tancred's office, at the Piccadilly end of the Haymarket, occupied the entire third floor of a large building. Philippa arrived at four o'clock in a mood far less optimistic than the one in which she had left Elcombe Grove. Getting into the elevator and pressing the button, she wondered whether she had been too impulsive. It was all very well to plan; it was Lord Tancred who would have to perform.

As the elevator went up, her spirits sank. She reminded herself that she was here because he was the only person she knew who had the power and the influence to carry out what she had in mind, but she could not prevent herself from recalling what had passed between them at their last meeting. The memory made her feel that it would be wise to stop the elevator, press the Down button and go home. They had parted on a very sour note; he had summarized her character in no complimentary terms, and she had been equally frank—far too frank, she now thought—about his failings. But that was a long time ago, and since then he had married and divorced a wife and it was not likely that he had had time to brood over a previous engagement. She was here in a good cause and he would at least have to listen. If he didn't choose to get involved—he used to have a gift, she recalled, for not getting involved—he'd no doubt be able to direct her to several other important people who could lend their support.

She stepped out of the elevator onto a wide, thickly carpeted corridor. Small green-and-gold chairs stood at intervals along the wall, flanking imposing double doors. She realized for the first time how far he had travelled, and how fast, from the small, bare office in which—how long ago?—he had interviewed her for the post of temporary secretary and said without conviction that she might do but she must understand that her appointment would come to an end as soon as his own secretary recovered from her illness. By the time the secretary had recovered, he had offered her a permanent post, and it had not been in his office.

She pushed open a door marked *Reception* and found herself in a sitting room carpeted in blue and curtained in bronze. At a spinet-shaped desk in one corner was a pretty girl, who greeted her with a smile.

"Good afternoon. May I help you?"

"Please. I'd like to speak to Lord Tancred."

The girl opened a large black book and turned its pages.

"Let me see. Here we are: today's appointments. May I know your name, please?"

"Miss Brackley."

"Miss . . . I'm so sorry, it's very odd, but I don't seem able to find your name down for this afternoon." She turned another page. "Have you perhaps made a mistake in the day?"

"I didn't make an appointment. It was silly of me, I suppose, but it didn't occur to me. I just dropped in for a talk. Is he in?"

The smile faded; a slight frown took its place.

"I'm afraid Lord Tancred never sees anybody without an appointment. Would you care to make one?"

"Yes. For this afternoon. He must be in—his car's outside, unless he's changed it since he last appeared in it in the papers."

"I don't know anything about his car, I'm afraid. Unless you make an appointment, Miss Brackley, it will be absolutely impossible for Lord Tancred to see you."

"Are you the last bastion?"

"The—?"

"Once I get past you, how many other holdups are there?"

"There are no holdups, Miss Brackley. Visitors who have appointments are checked by me, and I hand them over to Lord Tancred's assistant secretary."

"Then how about handing me over?"

"Quite, quite impossible."

"Look, don't be silly," Philippa entreated. "I know you're only doing what you understand to be your job, but there's no need to be too rigid. In fact, in my experience—and I've worked in an office, and for the same boss you're working for—rigidity never got you anywhere. I'm not here to bother Lord Tancred. He's a very old friend of mine. If you could get the news along the grapevine that Philippa Brackley had dropped in to see him, he might promote you."

"I'm afraid—"

"Why not let the assistant secretary do the worrying? Just hand me over and say I wouldn't listen to reason. Where does he lurk?"

The girl's eyes went involuntarily to a door behind Philippa.

"Oh, in there?"

"You can't . . . Miss Brackley, will you kindly . . . "

Philippa closed the door on the protests and found herself in a larger but less colourful room; the rugs and curtains were of sober hue and the young man seated at the desk was not pretty. Behind him was a door with glass panels, through which she could see four desks and four typists all busily at work.

"Good afternoon," Philippa said as he rose. "I came—"

"This lady," broke in the receptionist, who had entered on Philippa's heels, "has no appointment. I've explained to her that it's quite impossible for Lord Tancred to see anybody without an appointment."

"Quite right. Thank you, Miss Carmichael. I will deal with the matter."

"Good. It won't take you long," Philippa told him as Miss Carmichael withdrew. "I'm an old friend of Lord Tancred and all I want is twenty minutes' chat with him, that's all."

"As an old friend," the assistant secretary suggested smoothly, "it would have been wiser to telephone to Lord Tancred and ask him to let us know that you were coming. Without an appointment, and without any word from him, I'm afraid I—"

"Where there's an assistant," Philippa broke in, "there must be an assisted. He's the last impediment, I take it? Could you ask him to come and listen to me for a moment?"

"He is with Lord Tancred, I'm afraid, Miss . . . I didn't catch your name."

"Don't worry about my name. Just buzz the man you're supposed to assist, and tell him there's a crisis and he ought to come and help you out."

The young man stared at her for a moment—a long, measuring look. Then he opened the door behind him.

"Please come this way," he requested.

She followed him. He crossed the main office and ushered her into a room marked *Private*. It contained several comfortable armchairs, a cocktail cabinet and—in case, she thought, there was time to do any work—a large desk.

"Lord Tancred's secretary is busy," the young man told her, "but I will tell him that you are here."

He withdrew, closing the door behind him. She felt that she was getting closer; this was an executive's room. Tom had indeed made the grade—a vast change, this, from two rooms and a lavatory shared with the staff of the office on the floor below.

The door opened, and she turned. Before her was a man in his early forties. His glance was direct and cold, his voice even colder.

"I understand that you have demanded an interview with Lord Tancred," he said. "I have come to tell you that it is impossible for you to see him. He is, as you must be aware, an extremely busy man, and his time for receiving visitors is strictly limited. I will take your name and pass it to the receptionist and she will give you a day and time as—"

"Don't bother about that," Philippa interrupted. "Is Lord Tancred in?"

"For the moment, yes. He and I are—"

"Will you go and tell him that Philippa Brackley wants twenty minutes of his time? You may add that I've come in a spirit of friendship."

There was a pause. Philippa met and bore a hard, keen stare. At the end of it, he turned away, and she found herself alone once more. When he returned a few minutes later, he looked in better spirits; he was almost smiling.

"I'm sorry, Miss Brackley," he said. "As I informed you, Lord Tancred is too busy to see you. He sends his compliments and begs you to make an appointment for another day."

"Well, just take the compliments back," Philippa said, "and tell him that if he's busy, I'll wait. Tell him I'm in no hurry. If he's too busy today, I can come back tomorrow with sandwiches and coffee, and fill in time chatting with the staff and telling them what good friends he and I used to be when he came courting me. Tell him—"

She stopped. The secretary was no longer with her. She sat on one of the deep armchairs and with relief put down the bag in which she had placed the statuette; it was heavy. She was just leaning back and making herself comfortable when the secretary reappeared, his face a mask of disapprobation. Gazing at a point above her head, he announced in a chilling tone that Lord Tancred would give her a few minutes of his time.

She rose and followed him through a small anteroom. He knocked on a door, opened it, ushered her in, spoke her name and withdrew, closing the door behind him. From behind the desk rose a man of about forty-five, so long and so lean that the process was not so much rising as unfolding. He was sallow, with good features, and might have been thought handsome if his expression had been less forbidding. His haircut and his clothes were a successful compromise between what had been and what was to be in men's fashions. He motioned Philippa to a chair.

"Good afternoon, Philippa." His tone was polite, but far from warm. "I hope you're well?"

She sat down and gave him a frankly appraising look.

"Not an extra ounce," she commented.

His eyebrows went up.

"I'm afraid I can't say the same of you. You appear to have put on, if I may say so, a good deal of weight. But from what my secretary reported, you have not changed in any other way."

"I needed the weight; I was too bony. How are things with you, Tom? I can see the material side's all right. What I mean is, I hope you're happy."

"Very happy, thank you," he said stiffly. He seated himself but gave no other sign of relaxing. "And you?"

"Well, I go along as usual. I'm in business."

"Yes, I heard. A china shop, I understand."

"Sort of. If you'll drop in one day, I'll show you round, but make it fairly soon because I might be going out of business. You used to like china, if I—"

"Did you come here to talk about the past?"

She frowned.

"No, I didn't. But I haven't set eyes on you, or you on me, for a number of years, and I was trying to build a kind of bridge. Did you ever regret throwing me over?"

"It would be more accurate to say that you threw me over. May I inquire what brought you here this afternoon?"

"I came because I want something done, and you're the only person in the world—correction, the only person I know in the world—who can do it. You're the only person I'm remotely in touch with who can fix things at top level. And this problem I have can only be resolved right at the very top. We didn't want to fill the house with police inspectors asking silly questions and passing the answers on to the press. We wanted to keep the whole thing dead secret and—"

"Would you identify the 'we'?"

"Well, you remember I had a distant cousin by the name of Brooke?"

"You had a cousin named Edmund Brooke, to whom you were engaged before you became engaged to me."

"That's the one. If you remember, he married someone in Macau and she was killed in an accident in England less than two years after they were married. She was, as I think I once told you, actually driving up to Yorkshire to see me, that's to say my father and me, when the car crashed and—"

"I remember. So?"

"There was a little daughter named Vitorina, Tory for short. She and Edmund live with her Portuguese relations in Lisbon. She arrived here yesterday morning to go to a boarding school and I was to see her on to the school train, but she came out in spots and I had to ring the school and they said she couldn't go back without a doctor's say-so, and the doctor came and said—"

"Please!"

The word, the tone and Lord Tancred's upheld hand brought her to a halt, as they had so often done in the past. She looked irritated.

"If you're not even going to listen—"

"I will listen to a connected story. I will not listen to a rambling discourse. Will you kindly begin at the beginning, and give me, if you're capable of doing so, a coherent explanation. You said you came to ask me to do something for you. What is it? In a few words, if you please."

"Certainly. I'd like to begin by saying that success doesn't suit you; it's given you a magisterial manner. The way you are now, I've no hope that you'll listen with any kind of understanding or sympathy—but here it is. I have with me in this bag some stolen property of great value. I want you to see that it's restored to its owners in Lisbon. As far as I'm aware, this can only be done by asking one of your diplomatic friends to take it back in his Customs-immune bag, and that's what I came to ask you to arrange. There is no other way of dealing with the situation. Nothing will induce me to tell the police about this. You may have to, but if you do you'll be talking to somebody right at the top, the man who controls the entire police force and who can order things to be kept secret. So—"

"Stolen . . . Stolen by whom, may I ask? Or is that also to be kept secret?"

"Stolen by a man who offered himself as escort to Tory on the way from Lisbon to London, when the people she was supposed to be coming with couldn't travel. When or how he stole the statue nobody knows; that's for your friends to find out, if they can. I brought it because—"

"A statue? You brought a statue?"

"A statuette, if you're going to split hairs. I'll show you."

She lifted the bag she had placed on the rug beside her chair. From it she drew a bundle neatly swathed in a silk scarf. Unwinding the scarf, she placed the golden statuette on the desk before Lord Tancred, sat back and waited for his comments.

There were none. He had nothing to say. He could only look—a long, unbelieving look. Then his hands went out slowly, and he lifted the saint and drew it closer and continued to stare at it, turning it in his hands.

"So this is it . . . " he said at last.

"This is what? You mean you've seen it before?"

"No. I've heard of it. It was described to me by our last ambassador to Portugal. He told me about an extraordinary house in Lisbon with a chapel full of treasures that—"

"This is one of them. I can't tell you how it was—"

She stopped; Lord Tancred appeared to have forgotten her. He was passing a gentle finger over the statuette, admiring the exquisite workmanship.

"Look at those hands gripping the staff," he murmured. "And the child's hands and—"

"That's not a child. That's the Infant Jesus."

He withdrew his gaze from the statuette and fixed it on her.

"You said?"

"I was just telling you that it's Saint Christopher carrying the Infant Jesus across a river because there wasn't a bridge. When he was halfway across—"

"Thank you. I know the legend. This is in fact an allegory. Christopher means the bearer of Christ. The child was Christ. The river was the river of death."

"Thank *you*. That's just like you, always expert at changing a nice legend into a nasty allegory. I think the owners will go along with the legend, and so will I."

"What connection have you with the owners?" he asked.

"I told you—didn't you listen? They're the family Edmund married into. There were three daughters, and one of them married a man from Macau and went to live there. It was her daughter that Edmund married. It's her granddaughter that I'm talking about—Edmund's daughter, Tory. What else do you want to know?"

"Who is this man you accuse of the theft?"

"Accuse? He took that saint out of its niche in the chapel. He put it into Tory's luggage."

"Into . . . ?"

"Into Tory's luggage, to sneak it past the Customs at Hendaye. He knew quite well they wouldn't bother with a basket belonging to a schoolgirl, and he was right; they didn't. He was going to transfer it back to his own luggage, but it unaccountably vanished."

"The statuette?"

"I wish you'd *listen*. The statuette is standing on your desk. What disappeared was this man's luggage, and he went after it and hasn't been seen since, so when your friends have got the saint safely back in its place, they can start trying to find—"

"*Please!*"

She made an impatient sound. "Look, Tom, I know we're both some years older than we were, but you used at least to be able to follow anything one said to you. What's the matter now? I've told you the facts."

"But not in sequence. Will you please allow me to restate them clearly?"

"Go ahead."

"One: A man named—named what?"

"Darlan. I don't suppose for a moment it's his real—"

"A man named Darlan offered himself as escort to this child named Tory, who was coming to England to go to school. Was he a friend of the family?"

"No. Apparently Edmund used to meet him at the golf club in Estoril, and they used to go round the course together."

"Why should he come forward with an offer of escorting the child?"

"Child? Well, yes, I suppose ten is only a child, but it's funny, I don't think of her as a child, somehow. She was to travel with friends—a mother, and twin daughters who, like Tory, were coming to school in England. Not the same school, but the opening of terms happened to coincide, so the father started off by car with the heavy luggage, including Tory's, and Tory was to go by train with the wife and the twins. But the twins came out in spots and couldn't travel, and the next question you're going to ask—and for once it's a question that needs to be asked—is why her own father didn't come with her. One reason is that his job still takes him flying nonstop round the world, and he was on the point of taking off for Lima. The other reason is that since his wife's death he hasn't set foot in England. I wouldn't have said that Edmund was the type to let the past get a stranglehold on him, but that's what it appears to have done. His wife's name is never mentioned, and he still shirks coming back to the place where the accident happened. So that left this Darlan, who obviously saw his chance to get the statuette safely past the Customs and—"

"You said that he was not a friend of the family. Then how—"

"When he made his offer to act as escort, the old aunts invited him to dinner, and he was shown round, but that wasn't when he stole the statuette, because it was in its place when Mass was said in the chapel on the morning of Tory's departure. Then the old lady, by which I mean the oldest old lady, Tory's great-grandmother, name of Jesuina, pointed out that the saint had vanished, but nobody took any notice, because she's not quite right in the head, poor old thing, and has taken to hiding objects and pretending they're lost, and the only thing that puzzled them this time was not where she'd put it but how she could have reached up to its niche and got it down. It weighs . . . well, you can pick it up and guess what it weighs. Will you get one of your diplomatic friends to take it back to Lisbon?"

"Most certainly not."

"Why not?" she demanded.

"Because, in the first place, it would be a highly dishonest act to conceal—"

"How else do you suggest getting it back? If it isn't taken or sent back, think what'll happen: old Jesuina'll die of frustration because she knows she hasn't taken it but nobody will believe her. The aunts will grow agitated and begin to accuse the servants, and—"

"—and the police will be called, and the child's story investigated."

"No. Never, never, *never*. Tory is *not* going to be dragged into this. Why make such a fuss about asking one of your diplomat friends to do a simple thing like this? You can assure him that—"

"I could assure him of nothing. I could give him no assurance whatsoever. This whole tale is absurd. It doesn't hang together. You stated, for example, that the man Darlan was the thief. You next said that his luggage disappeared, and he with it. What we're left with is a story told you by a child ten years old. If the statuette was in its niche on the morning of her journey to England, how could the man Darlan have stolen it? I take it that the house and the chapel aren't open to any chance comer?"

"No. There's a guard on the gate—at least, on the gate that opens from the road onto a courtyard outside the chapel. But—"

"Throughout the story, there is not a shadow of proof that this man is implicated."

"Didn't he put the thing into Tory's basket, the one she left behind at Austerlitz?"

"She left—?"

"She left it in the station cloakroom after she'd had a wash. She'd taken the statuette out in the train."

"So she says."

"Don't be silly, Tom, for heaven's sake! How else could she have got hold of the man's shirt?"

"Shirt? This is the first mention of—"

"He wrapped it in his shirt before putting it into the basket."

"You have the shirt?"

"No. She gave it away."

"Ah. To whom?"

"To a Portuguese immigrant on the train."

"And you believe this extraordinary sequence of mischances? You believe that a man offered himself as escort, stole this statuette, wrapped it in a shirt and put it into her basket to get it through Customs, and then vanished, taking his luggage but leaving the statuette behind? Can you seriously expect me to go with a fairy tale of this kind to any intelligent or responsible person?"

"You mean you don't believe a single word of what I've told you?"

"I believe that you believe all you have told me."

"But you don't?"

"I find it garbled and totally unconvincing. There are too many unrelated facts. Some of the facts, in fact all the facts, require checking."

"So how do you propose to check them?"

"By seeing, by questioning this child. Until I do that, I shall approach nobody and promise nothing. Once again, as so often in the past, you have acted on impulse and gotten yourself into an impossible position. Once again, as always in the past, you have allowed your emotions—your heart, if you like—to overrule whatever intelligence you have. The child has told you a story to account for her possession of this statuette, and you have believed everything she has told you. I do not. There are some angles that look to me extremely suspicious. If I may meet her and question her, I shall be able to form an opinion as to how much truth—if any—there is in her story. Until then, you must understand that I cannot involve myself in the matter."

"Well, see her and talk to her. When? And don't say next week, because this is urgent. That man Darlan is roaming round loose, remember."

"Is the child at your house?"

"Yes. When will you talk to her?"

"Now, if you wish."

"I take back anything I ever said against you. Until you decide what's to be done, would you put Saint Christopher somewhere safe?"

112

"I shall certainly keep it here until this matter is settled."

He rose, picked up the statuette and walked across the room to a small safe. Opening it, he placed the saint inside. Then he pressed a button on his desk.

"Miss Peters," he asked the girl who answered the summons, "will you please take this lady to the waiting room? I will be ready to go with you in twenty minutes," he told Philippa. He halted her as she reached the door. "One moment. I suppose you will be able to give me an address at which I can reach Tory's father?"

She stared at him in blank amazement.

"What on earth has Tory's father got to do with this?" she inquired.

"The responsibility is his, not yours. He will have to come to England and shoulder it."

"Come to . . . A lot of help you're being." She spoke in disgust, and the waiting Miss Peters looked nervous. "What do you suppose Tory's father . . . And what's Tory going to say if I tell her that you're summoning him? She'd probably rather have the police."

"She may find herself dealing with both. Kindly accompany Miss Peters."

He joined her, as he had promised, at the end of twenty minutes and led her out to the elevator through a series of doors held open by respectful members of his staff. Beside the pavement waited his large, chauffeur-driven car. Into this he handed her.

"Nice," she commented, settling herself against the cushions, "but not as roomy as the bus I usually travel on. Do you remember your first car, Tom, that awful one that was always breaking down and leaving us stranded without a hope of getting a bed for the night?"

"No." With resignation, he noted the chauffeur's twitching ears, but he knew from experience that it would be no use pointing out to her that they had an audience. "When did you move back to London?"

"After my father died. I would have come direct from the funeral if I could, because I was so sick of moors, but I had to wait until I could sell the house. It wasn't easy to find a buyer; you'd be surprised how many people don't want a house stuck in the sticks, with high ceilings and no heating. Look, Tom, you're not going to put on one of your cross-examining acts for Tory, are you?"

"I shall ask questions. I have no intention of frightening her."

"You won't frighten her. In my opinion, she's unfrightenable. In many ways, she's like her father. You never liked him much, did you?"

"No. But I never really knew him. In what way is she like him?"

"Well, sort of controlled. Outwardly she's small and thin and very, very polite—she's got beautiful manners, which makes her sound out of step with the times, but they suit her. She listens, but she doesn't talk much. People might think she was dull, but she isn't. I find myself talking to her as I'd talk to you. She doesn't give out much, but she takes in. When you come to think of it, it must have been a pretty dreary life for her, brought up by those old women and followed about by a sort of retired governess. I asked her how many servants there were, and she said not many and then reeled off the names of about a couple of dozen, and that didn't include the one who guards the chapel gate and the several who weed the garden. Can a child brought up like that, in this day and age, help being unusual?"

"I suppose not. She's Catholic, I presume?"

"Every second week. Edmund seems to have stepped in and injected some Protestantism somewhere around her seventh birthday."

"Too late. Has she much affection for her great-aunts?"

"None that shows. I think the one she really likes is Jesuina, who's currently supposed to have hidden the golden saint. I think you could take away the house and its contents and the aunts and the governess and the retainers, and leave Jesuina and the chapel, and Tory would be content."

"You exclude her father?"

"He excluded himself."

"He can't be blamed, can he, if his work takes him away a good deal?"

"Of course he can be blamed. He's not an office boy, is he? The matter of where he travels, or whether he travels, is entirely in his own hands. I think you're crazy to haul him here, but if he does come, it'll be a pleasure to tell him what I think of his record as a father. Here we are," she said as the chauffeur turned into Elcombe Grove and slowed down to glance at the numbers of the houses. "The end one," she told him.

She led Lord Tancred to the door; before they reached it, it had been opened by Tory.

"Hello, Tory. I've brought a friend—the one I told you about." Philippa led the way into the sitting room. "This is Lord Tancred. Tom, this is Tory. Don't go away, Tory, he wants to talk to you. Tom, can we offer you tea, or a drink?"

"Neither, thank you."

"Then sit over there. He's put Saint Christopher in his safe, Tory, and what he's here for is to check up on a few points before sending out the secret police to arrest this Darlan, and without dragging us into a sordid session with so-called detectives. Come and sit beside me on the sofa. Tom, you can begin."

He did not begin at once. He was still standing. Tory was seated, her hands folded on her lap; thus, Philippa thought, she must have listened to the old aunts. And no sign of nervousness, though that grave, almost accusing look on Lord Tancred's face would have sent a chill through most children. He was doing his best to appear fatherly, she knew—but fatherliness didn't come naturally to him, and he would do much better to stop trying to be anything but his usual serious, stern-but-just self.

He took a chair and addressed Tory.

"All I want," he told her, "are a few facts. Perhaps you've already discovered that Philippa has a way of saying a good deal without making her meaning clear? She has spoken of statuettes and travelling companions and missing luggage and Portuguese immigrants; I'm here to disentangle the facts, because until I get a clear picture of how that valuable statuette changed its place from a Lisbon chapel to my London office I can't be of any help. As an old friend of Philippa, I would like to help if I can, but this would

115

involve asking certain friends to assist me, and that I won't do until I have satisfied myself that I know exactly what happened on your journey to England. Do I make myself clear?"

"Yes."

Clear, and quite, quite unnecessarily pompous, Philippa thought, and felt again the mixture of affection and irritation he had always inspired in her. He was so good, so generous—and so stiff-necked. He distrusted levity, loathed flippancy. He was honest and staunch and at rare moments he could be fun, but he couldn't bring himself to be lighthearted. Why didn't he sit back and ask Tory to tell the story in her own words? But Lord Tancred preferred his own method of cross-examination. His questions were crisp and searching. Tory's answers were calm and truthful. Only when question and answer had reached the final point was it necessary for her to use caution.

"And what did you intend to do with the statuette?"

"I hoped I'd be able to hide it somewhere until I could take it back to Portugal with me."

"And what made you change your plan?"

Tory hesitated. So far, the truth had been all she needed to tell. But now the truth would not serve, for the truth was that she had found in Philippa, unexpectedly, a person on whom she could utterly rely. To say so would sound unconvincing—and in any case she could not decide what words she would use. Love and trust? Meeting Lord Tancred's cold, clear, searching gray eyes, she decided not to mention love or trust.

"I thought Philippa might keep it for me until I came back from school," she said.

"A rather heavy responsibility to place on her, wouldn't you say?"

For the first time, Philippa spoke.

"My shoulders are broad," she said, "but yours are broader, and that's why we chose you to take the weight." She saw him rising to his feet, and spoke with relief. "Have you finished with Tory?"

"For the moment, yes. I asked you for an address, if you remember."

She went to the desk in the corner, wrote the single word *Lima* on it, folded it and handed it to him.

"Why don't you send your car away and let your chauffeur find himself a meal while you stay and have supper with us?" she asked. "Or if you want to eat out, we'll treat you to sandwiches at the milk bar."

He declined both these invitations, said good-bye to Tory and followed Philippa to the front door.

"So you see," she said, as he put on his overcoat, "it's just as I told you. Now all you have to do is—"

"I must think it over."

He had opened the front door and stepped outside. She took a few steps and spoke with a frown.

"What's there to think over?"

"A great many things. The first essential is to get her father here. It's out of the question to proceed further without making the facts known to him."

"Well, it's on that paper: you'll have to look in Lima. But he doesn't stay anywhere for long."

"I shall find him."

"What are you going to do—scare him by mentioning thieves and—"

"He'll be told enough to get him here. Why did you avoid telling her that I was going to send for her father?"

"I hoped you'd change your mind."

He spoke in an exasperated voice.

"Can't you see that this is a serious matter? Don't you understand that this story has to be investigated? If it's true, we're dealing with what may prove to be an international gang of thieves. If it's not true, it'll be her father's responsibility to find out why she lied."

"You still think Tory's been telling lies?"

"No. I think she told the truth."

"But—"

"But not by any means the whole truth."

He was striding towards his car. She closed the door and returned to the sitting room to find Tory standing thoughtfully by the table. She decided to speak without preliminaries.

"Lord Tancred's bringing your father to England, Tory."

Tory turned to look at her. There was dismay on her face, but no sign of any dawning pleasure.

"Bringing him here? Why?"

"Something to do with shouldering responsibility. In other words, Lord Tancred thinks he ought to be here while these inquiries are going on."

"But all the way from Lima . . . "

"Distance is no obstacle. Don't forget that Lord Tancred's operating on a very high level. You and I, if we thought your father ought to be here—which we don't—would have sent a telegram saying: Come. There won't be a telegram; there'll be an order to an influential official, British, who'll locate your father and dispatch him."

"But when he gets here, what can he do?"

"It isn't so much a matter of what he does; it's a matter of who he is: your father, responsible for you. All you and I thought of was how to get Saint Christopher back to Lisbon, but, as Lord Tancred points out, that's not the whole of it. Your father placed you in the care of a man who turned out to be a thief. You're lucky he was only a thief; he might have been . . . well, never mind about that. Having got you into this, your father's got to be around to see what can be done about laying hands on Darlan."

"But Lord Tancred can do more than my father to . . . Can't he?"

"If he wants to. As I told you, he's Lord God Almighty, but, like Lord God Almighty, he doesn't always latch on at once to what it was you asked him to do. One of the things you and I hoped for was secrecy—just you and me and Lord Tancred and a couple of ambassadors or chiefs of police. But he seems to think that your father's a key man, so he'll be here as soon as they can put him on a plane, and I think he'll be completely useless, or possibly even obstructive, but it'll be nice to see him. And he needed a bomb under him to make him aware of his parental duties; maybe this is it."

"Anyway, he'll believe me. Lord Tancred didn't."

"He half did. He thinks you left out bits which you thought didn't matter, but which might be important. He's anxious to get everything straight, so try to remember any details about Darlan that you'd dismissed as trivial."

"When will my father arrive?"

"Some time tomorrow, I suppose. There's several hours' difference between our time and Lima time, but I can't work out whether that speeds him up or slows him down. There certainly won't be any time lost in getting him off; if there isn't a plane going at once, they'll borrow one from the nearest President. Shall we make ourselves supper at home, or would you rather go out and eat?"

"Let's stay here."

"Got any plans for tomorrow morning?"

"I'll go and see if Derek brings Leo to the waste ground, and play with them. I'd like a dog like Leo. Does this school allow pets?"

"In my day, they stretched to a guinea pig or two, but drew the line at cats or dogs or tigers. Did you have any pets in Portugal?"

"No."

"Why not?"

"My aunts don't like animals much."

"I see. I wonder what animals, if asked, would say about your aunts? Come and pour me out a drink, and open yourself a Coke or something, and then let's drink to the safe return of Saint Christopher."

Chapter Six

Tory woke next morning to find that Philippa had already left the house. She had a bath, and lay for some time in the water trying, unsuccessfully, to imagine her father's reactions at being summoned to England. Then she dressed and went down to make her breakfast, after which she tried out some of the household equipment. She began with the vacuum cleaner; then she put two of her blouses into the washing machine, transferred them to the spin drier and after that ironed them, and at the end of her labours decided somewhat prematurely that housework presented no problems provided that there were enough labour-saving devices.

It was eleven o'clock when she had finished her work, and she decided to go out and look for Derek and his dog. The day looked warm—there was sun slanting in through the window of the sitting room, and the trees in the school grounds opposite were motionless, which meant that the wind, which yesterday had seemed to be blowing straight off the Polar ice, had died down. But when she went outside and walked to the corner of the road, she found that an English January sun was not the January sun she had known in Lisbon. This one gave light but no heat.

The waste ground that morning could well have been called a

recreation ground; there were school parties playing soccer and handball and basketball, ponies trotting round and round an improvised arena, on their backs juvenile riders in various stages of proficiency, from knee-grippers to mane-clingers. Scouts were taking compass bearings; around or between all these groups were dog-owners exercising their pets. Tory could not see Derek or Leo, but she noticed close to Philippa's garden wall the two boys who had thrown rubbish into the garden the day before. They were kneeling in the wet mud, hammering and digging, and as she drew nearer she saw that it was not Philippa's wall but the wall of the house next door at which they were working; as it had been made too high for them to throw things over it, she concluded, they were planning to push things under it. She stood watching them for a time, and then turned to see Derek and Leo coming towards her. Leo, recognizing her, without hesitation came bounding up; she bent and lifted him into her arms and stood trying to keep her face out of reach of his eager tongue. Derek's greeting was laconic.

" 'Lo."

"Hello." She put the dog on the ground. "Did you bring a ball?"

He produced the tennis ball, and for some time they played with it, and, as on the day before, it was Leo who decided when the game had gone on long enough.

"Where you going now?" Derek asked. "Back to number fourteen?"

"I don't know. You could come with me if you wanted to."

"No. Too near old mother Dexter. You can come home with me, only I don't suppose you want to see Mrs. T. anymore. She said to bring you. Want to go?"

"Yes."

He looked puzzled.

"Can't see why. All she does is talk, talk, talk."

"And knit."

"Those scarves? Know why she does those? When she feels nosy, she goes round the houses with 'em in a bag, selling 'em. A lot of the people feel sorry for her, and some of 'em ask her to go inside, and they might even give her a drink, and then she gets to know all about them, and that's what she's really after. Did she string you on with a lot of gup about when she was an actress?"

"No."

"Well, she wasn't. She did a bit on the stage with old Ernie Barlow, but that was only because he was sorry for her and tried to make her better herself. He was nobody, just like Mrs. T., my mum said, but he practiced talking, practiced and practiced, and now you can't tell the difference, but with Mrs. T., she had to keep trying, and when he's not there she forgets. And she doesn't know much about real actors and actresses, except that she worked in theaters. Know who her father was?"

"No."

"Stage-door keeper. He had eight kids, and Mrs. T. was one of 'em. Her brothers got to be stagehands. Mrs. T. was all sorts of things, dresser, or showing people to their seats, or doing the ironing backstage. She knew my grandfather and my father, and my mum says they asked her to the wedding when they got married, my mum and dad I mean, because she'd been at my dad's christening, and they'd been running into each other in theaters ever since. That's why my mum roomed with her when we came to London, but she was sorry when she found out how dirty the house was, except on Thursdays."

"What's different on Thursdays?"

"You'll see when we get there. She doesn't do anything all the rest of the week, nothing, not even wash up, but every Thursday she gets up at six and starts. Makes a job of it. Goes through every room, takes her all morning and then she's through until the next Thursday."

He stopped to put the leash on Leo; his conversation then turned to racing cars, television personalities, pop groups and soccer teams, and he paused only when he had assured himself of her total ignorance of any or all the topics.

"Do you like your stepfather?"

"Yes, I do. I liked him first when I was coming out of school one day, and that Mrs. Dexter was passing, going to her house, and some boys called her names and then they ran away, and she saw my stepfather coming out of the school gate, only he wasn't my stepfather then, he hadn't even met my mum, and Mrs. Dexter said it was me who'd called her names, and he must have heard and she wanted to give his name to the police as a witness. And he told her to go home and stop trying to trap little boys, and I thought it was nice of him to say that, only she's had it in for me worse than for the other boys round here ever since then. She hates me the worst. She said if she ever sees Leo in her garden she'll have him destroyed."

"Have him what?"

"Destroyed. She'll take him to the vet to be put down."

"To be what?"

"Put down, put down, put down. Destroyed. Given an injection to finish him off."

"She . . . she'd do that?"

"You bet she would. Ask anyone. They all know her round here. If you ask me, she's the one who ought to be put down." They turned into Colony Street, and he stopped at the door of a shop. "Wait for me. I'm going to buy something to eat."

She waited, looking at the trays of ready-cooked meats laid out on trays in the window. She saw Derek indicate the kinds he wanted, and several slices of ham and brawn and sausage were placed in greaseproof paper, wrapped up and handed to him. He rejoined Tory, and they walked the rest of the way to Mrs. Tesworth's rooms.

Before Tory had got halfway down the iron steps, she could smell the soap and the disinfectant that Mrs. Tesworth had been using during her morning's cleaning. The yard had been scrubbed, the trash cans emptied and lined up in military precision. The dark passage smelt of strong carbolic acid; the strip of carpet that had lain on it had been removed and cleaned and now hung over a chair, ready to be put down again when the floor was dry. The open doors showed a tidy bedroom and a neat kitchen. Behind the curtain, newly dusted, was a room smelling of polish. The sagging photographs on the walls had been given new sticky paper; the large cupboard in one corner had been moved to one side, and behind it Tory saw a bed, proving that this was Mrs. Tesworth's room by night as well as by day.

Mrs. Tesworth, loudly declaring herself exhausted, was unwinding a scarf from her head.

"Done in, I am. Come in, Tory, my dear. Derek, you turn off that telly, d'you hear. I'm going to sit down and have a bit o' quiet. Go on, turn it off."

Derek, who had just succeeded in finding a program he liked, switched off the set and spoke mutinously.

"What's the idea? I want to look."

"Well, I don't. Besides, there's visitors. Where's your manners?"

"If I can't watch here," he said, "then I'll go up the street and watch Mr. Barlow's. Come on, Leo."

The door banged behind him. Mrs. Tesworth sank into the largest chair and gave a sigh.

"Just like 'is dad, always goes straight after anything he wants," she commented. "I used to like it in 'is dad, so I suppose I can't grumble when young Derek starts it. Got to thinking about his mum today, while I was cleaning out, and wondering 'ow she was going to like livin' away from the theater. She's part of it, same as I've always been. 'Er mother, all 'er sisters, both 'er aunts, 'er granddad—all in it. Not on the stage, none of 'em—but theater, just the same. There's a lot more than what the audience sees. It's nice to go out there and stand and say 'Friends, Romans' and all the rest, but before you can 'ave that, there's scenery and there's costumes and there's props and there's prompts and there's callboys and Gawd knows what. That's what I've been part of the 'ole of me life. I'm seventy-six, and look it, and I don't know much about what they teach in schools, but you ask any of the old stage'ands, if you can find any today, and ask if they remember Mrs. T., and see what they say. I've seen actors and actresses go up and come down; they'd be in work, or out of work—restin'. Not us. You take a look at all them faces in them snaps I've got up on the walls. Stayers, year in and year out, and most of 'em—like me—old Londoners. You cold, ducks? Bring your chair closer to the fire. I turn it off the day I clean the place out, so I shouldn't be surprised if you feel the room cold. What was I talkin' about?"

"London."

"Well, not this London. The London I knew, that's dead 'n gone. Why should you want to set there listenin' to an old woman gassin' on about what's dead 'n gone?"

"I like listening."

"I can see that. All I can't see is why."

"I like knowing about people."

"My sort of people?"

"Any sort of people. I mean, their real lives."

"Well, this was real enough. Gas lamps, we 'ad. All down our street of a Saturday night there was stalls with flares lightin' 'em, and the people behind 'em shoutin' out what they was sellin', and you could 'ardly 'ear 'em when the trams went clangin' by. I used to go out for my mum and buy forty oranges for a bob. I used to like foggy nights, with the shop lights shinin' out and all the people 'appy in the pubs. Young Derek grouses because 'e's asked to go out and buy 'imself a bit of this or that, but at 'is age all I wanted was to be sent out to buy myself some pease puddin' and a nice saveloy. I can still taste 'em, hot and peppery and full of lovely grease. There's no Cockneys now, no real ones like there used to be. It's not natural, like when I was young; it's all actin' nowadays, all put on. They've taken away all the old London, the London I was born in. I suppose they know what they're doin'. Whole streets—the street my mum was born in, gone. I can remember my old grandmum goin' up it in her old felt slippers with 'er 'air in papers and a jug in 'er 'and, on 'er way to the pub for some beer. You got a grandmum?"

"No. She died. I've got a great-grandmother."

"She'll miss you, I daresay. You been to boardin' school before?"

"No."

"Think you're goin' to like it?"

"I don't know."

"You've got a good many years to go on learnin' in. I never thought much about anythin' like that, not until I came across Mr.

Barlow. That was the first time I met anyone who'd started off like me, Cockney to the bone, and who'd taught himself a lot, 'ow to talk proper, 'ow to be'ave, things like that. There's a lot you can learn from the telly, but there's more in books, Mr. Barlow always says. I suppose you think I'm an ignorant old woman, and o' course I am, but I've come a long way. You 'ave to measure from where you started, don't you? From where I started to where I am now—that's a long way."

Listening, Tory forgot to keep track of time; when she left, it was so late that she had to run almost all the way to the milk bar. Philippa was waiting for her at the entrance.

"Tory"—she spoke at once—"your father phoned from the airport. He's arrived. I told him I'd send you to the house to wait for him. I can't go with you—I've got to go back to the shop for a little while, but I won't be long. You and he and I are going to have lunch together. You'd better go straightaway. Take a taxi, or he'll get to the house before you."

Edmund Brooke had arrived an hour earlier. He was met at the airport by Lord Tancred; their handshake was brief and cool. While they waited for the formalities of arrival to be concluded, Edmund made a telephone call to Philippa. Then he walked with Lord Tancred to the exit, carrying his suitcase.

"Can you give me some idea of what this is all about?" he asked.

Lord Tancred waited until they were in his car, which he was driving himself.

"How much did they tell you over there?" he asked.

"They said that my daughter had got involved with someone who was suspected of having stolen something, and it would be as well if I came and—their term—assumed responsibility. Thank you for all the trouble you went to to get me here. I haven't worked out how you came into it."

"Philippa came to my office."

"Couldn't she have got in touch with me?"

"She'd thought up a scheme. She was after two things: absolute secrecy, and the return of the stolen object to Portugal by way of a diplomatic bag. She approached me because she said I was the one person she knew who could see that the matter was kept secret, and who could find a handy diplomatic bag."

"Practical," Edmund commented. "Can you give me the details?"

"Your daughter, Tory, travelled with a man named Darlan. I understand that you didn't know him well. Tory arrived with an object of considerable value in her luggage, and claims that it was stolen by Darlan from the chapel of her great-grandmother's house in Lisbon."

"Stolen from the . . . But Darlan never went near the chapel."

"He was shown round the house, wasn't he?"

"Yes. I'd forgotten. He was."

"According to Tory, he was invited to the house only after he had offered himself as escort. He may or may not have had any previous idea of theft in his mind, but he would certainly have known that there was a chapel, and that it contained objects of value."

"What does Tory accuse him of stealing?"

"A good statuette of a saint carrying—"

"My God! Not Saint Christopher?"

"Yes. I wish I owned it. It's one of the most beautiful things I've ever seen."

"The Saint Christopher! But how . . . Wait a minute; I've remembered something. It was missing on the morning Tory left. It was assumed that her great-grandmother had hidden it, but she couldn't possibly have got at it and lifted it down. I ought to have made that clear at the time, but I didn't give the matter much attention."

"Do you know for certain that when he was shown round the house, the tour included the chapel?"

"It must have done. Tory's aunts took him round; I didn't go with them. But he couldn't have got in to steal anything. He would have been seen by the servants if he tried to get in by way of the house, and he couldn't get in from the side road to the chapel because there's a guard at that gate. You say that Tory definitely accuses him of having stolen the statuette?"

"Yes. If her story is true, he must have offered to travel with her in order to use her as cover to get the saint past the French Customs at Hendaye. He entered her compartment shortly before they arrived there, and asked her if she would mind his putting into her basket a shirt which he'd had difficulty in packing in his own luggage. He wrapped the statuette in the shirt, and—presumably because Tory would have noticed the greatly increased weight—carried the basket himself through Customs and into the Paris train."

"When did she find the statuette?"

"After Darlan left the train at Bayonne."

Edmund turned to stare at him.

"Darlan left the train?"

"Yes—in what I must say I find somewhat peculiar circumstances. According to Tory, he disembarked when the train stopped at Bayonne, telling her he was going to buy something that would relieve his headache. When he returned, he discovered that his luggage was no longer on the rack of the compartment. He left the train again, chasing a porter who was wheeling away a wagon, and missed the train. Tory went on alone to England."

"Alone? They were to meet Darlan's sister in Paris."

"Tory met her. She told Tory that she was not Darlan's sister."

"Good God!" He sat in thought for some moments. "You said the circumstances were peculiar. Why?"

"First, the fact that he could step off the train, however bad his headache, leaving that statuette in a basket, hidden only by a shirt. Next, the fact that Tory was standing, by her own admission, close to the door of the compartment, but saw nothing and heard nothing of the luggage being removed."

"Are you suggesting she hasn't told the truth?"

"I think that what she told me is true as far as it goes—but I feel certain that there are some facts which, unconsciously or deliberately, she hasn't mentioned."

"Does Philippa think that, too?"

"No. As usual, Philippa takes a line of her own. One of the most curious aspects of the matter is the fact that Tory said nothing whatsoever of any of this to Philippa when she arrived."

"She arrived with chicken pox. Philippa sent me a cable."

"It was a false alarm. But if it hadn't been, wouldn't you think that, feeling ill, there would be all the more reason for a child to want to confide in someone? But Tory said nothing at all until the following day." He accelerated and beat the red traffic light. "I don't find it easy to put to Philippa any doubts I feel about Tory's story, but I'll be more frank with you. An impersonal view might be that Tory, leaving home for the first time, leaving everything that was familiar and coming to a strange country to enter a strange school . . . wouldn't you agree that she might perhaps on an impulse have decided to take with her something to remind her of her home?"

"No. I wouldn't agree at all."

"I used the word 'impersonal,' " Lord Tancred said dryly. "She might have intended to—"

"You mean to say that she would have made up a pack of lies to account for being in possession of the statuette?"

"The word is still 'impersonal.' "

"The word is 'impossible.' Tory couldn't have done it. She couldn't have removed the statue from the chapel in the first place without being seen. She wouldn't have minded leaving the house. She wouldn't have minded leaving her great-aunts. I don't think, God help me, that she much minded leaving me. She certainly minded leaving her great-grandmother, and she certainly minded leaving the chapel, every part of which she loves. I don't know whether I can make you understand that she regards it with a kind of religious feeling—which at the same time isn't a feeling of awe or even of belief in anything the chapel or its contents stand for. She loves it because she has a feeling for beauty, and it's beautiful. She couldn't—I ask you to take my word for this—she couldn't remove the most valuable object in the chapel, put it into her suitcase, and bring it to England. She's an unusual child in many ways, and I don't understand many things about her, but I know some things with certainty, and I know that she couldn't and wouldn't have smuggled that statuette out of Portugal."

"Then I'll leave you to try to get the full story out of her. We shall see if you're left, as I was left, with a feeling that there was a piece missing. Perhaps she will tell you why she left her basket at Austerlitz. The reason she gives is that she didn't need it anymore, but she's clever enough to have realized that in leaving it in the cloakroom, empty, and telling this pseudo-sister of Darlan's that it was there, she hit on a very successful way of confusing the issue. The shirt she gave away, she says, to a Portuguese immigrant on the train. If Darlan is a thief, this woman—Madame Leblanc—is certainly his accomplice. I've given you the outline; I'll leave you to get what you can out of Tory. Would you mind if I dropped you at a taxi stand? I've an important appointment for lunch and I'm late."

"Put me out where you like. I'm very grateful for all you've done." The car stopped; he got out, took his suitcase and signalled a taxi. "Thanks again."

When he arrived at Philippa's house and rang the doorbell, the door was opened by Tory. There was a slight pause as they studied one another, and then she made an odd little gesture of invitation.

"Hello, Daddy. Please come in."

She closed the door behind him, held up her face for his kiss and waited for him to hang up his coat. Then she ushered him into the sitting room and indicated a chair.

"That's the most comfortable one," she said.

"Oh, is it? They all look as though I'd sink right through them. What kind of decor would you call this—futuristic?"

"Philippa likes the colours. Did you have a good journey?"

"I don't remember." He sat down and looked at her as she stood close beside him. "I don't remember, because I was thinking of you. I seem to have landed you into quite a lot of trouble. I'm sorry. I should have inquired a good deal more about Mr. Darlan before closing with his offer. I've heard part of the story from Lord Tancred—he met me at the airport, which was kind of him. How about telling me the rest of it? Or the whole thing from the beginning?"

"Wouldn't you like a drink of anything first?"

"I can't think of anything I'd like more. Has Philippa given you the run of the bar?"

"I know where everything is. In the kitchen."

"Can I mix it myself?"

"Of course you can."

By the time he was back in his chair, a drink beside him, Tory on the sofa facing him, the tension of the meeting had eased. She was sitting in an attitude that was familiar to him—ankles crossed, hands resting motionless in her lap. What was she feeling? he wondered. What was she thinking? He had been brought thousands of miles—to help her? How did he begin? The stiffness, the awkwardness of their meeting just now had brought home to him, with a force that shook him, his inadequacy as a parent. She had shown none of the emotion that a child, after such an experience, could have been expected to feel: relief at his arrival, eagerness to pour out her adventures. Above all, there had been not the smallest sign that she was glad to see him. He realized with a sinking feeling that he knew almost nothing about her—his own daughter. They might have been strangers meeting for the first time.

"Well, Tory," he prompted. "Let's begin at the beginning."

She told him the story as she had told it to Philippa; she added her answers to the questions that Lord Tancred has asked. Edmund listened without interrupting. When she ended, she sat waiting quietly for his comments, and, waiting, she began to sense something of what he was thinking, and felt sorry for him. She knew what he wanted, what they all wanted: They wanted not only the facts but her reaction to the facts. To satisfy them, she would have to tell them that she had moved her luggage, and she would have to tell them why. She would have to describe the dinner on the train, describe the half-drunk man sitting opposite to her and pressing her hand in his. That was what she should have told them. That was what she would never tell them, never tell anybody. If she told them, which she would not and could not, they would assume that she had been frightened. None of them would be able to understand that all she had felt was disgust and loathing. Could anybody of her age, she wondered, ever make grown-ups see the real truth? They called her a little girl; that, of course, was all she was: a little girl. Little girls were expected to be frightened of bad men. Everybody would understand that, but nobody would believe that a little girl wouldn't be frightened but would feel sickened and outraged by the touch of a slimy hand pressing hers. Disgust and outrage were reactions reserved for grown-ups. If she expressed them, she would be suspected of showing off, or of exaggerating, or of making it all up. And they would be upset if she told them another truth: that she would rather let Mr. Darlan go unpunished than to have to recall him to mind, have to remember him, see him, hear him, smell him. She had put him out of her mind and she did not want him brought back.

For the first time in her life, she saw—perhaps by the light that Philippa had shone on her father—that her own inability, her own disinclination to lay bare her feelings, was inherited from him. She had not learned how to keep things to herself; she had been born with the inclination and the ability. As he was, so was she. On entering the house, he had been unable to make any gesture of warmth or love or affection. He wanted to—this she suddenly knew with certainty—but he was unable to, for the reasons that she had been unable to reveal all that had passed between herself and Mr. Darlan. He might try to find words, but words wouldn't come—or he thought, as she was thinking, that the words might be misinterpreted. He was like her. More accurately, she was like him. They were the same, and it was strange that being so much alike hadn't seemed to bring them any closer together.

She saw that he was about to break the silence—but before he could speak they heard the sound of a key in the front door. It opened, closed with a crash, and the next moment Philippa was in the room.

"Edmund! I can't believe it!"

He went across the room and she took his hands and looked up at him with frank affection.

"It's lovely to see you again. Kiss me."

He bent and kissed her on both cheeks.

"It's been a long time," he said.

She had stepped back and was inspecting him from head to foot.

"You're wider than you were," she told him. "Unless it's just the contrast with Tom Tancred's long-and-lean look. Apart from that, you look just the same. Has Tory been telling you all about everything?

"Yes."

"Wasn't it bright of me to call in Tom to help us?"

"It was inspired."

"Tory, you're looking pale. Has your father been bullying you?"

"No."

"If he ever tries it, let me know. He or anyone else. Edmund, why, why, *why* didn't you tell her that we were engaged all those years ago? How could you send her to me without giving her any kind of . . . of *link?* Why didn't you—" She pulled herself up. "First things first. Did Tory offer you a drink? Yes, I see she did. Tory, I'd like one, please. I need one. Seeing your father again has made me feel very shaky. Slices of lemon, please, and tonic water out of the fridge, and ice and the bottle of Martini and anything you want for yourself, and open a can of nuts and a bottle of olives, and we'll all settle down to a pre-lunch drinking session before making your father take us to an expensive restaurant. Now Edmund," she continued, as Tory went to the kitchen, "tell me what Tom said to you."

"He seemed to think that the facts don't hang together very well."

"What he thought was that Tory hadn't told him the whole story. You've got to make him believe that she did."

"It isn't exactly a matter of what he believes. He's got to pass the facts on and what are the facts? That is, what are the facts as he sees them? A little girl arrives carrying a statuette and says that Mr.

Darlan wrapped it in his shirt and put it into her basket. There is no shirt. There is no basket. There is not even Mr. Darlan. Did Mr. Darlan leave this statuette wrapped in his shirt and leave the train long enough to miss it altogether? Was there, therefore, something in his suitcases of greater value than the statuette? Is there—"

"That's all very well, but—"

"Wait a minute. Tancred has to be responsible for any story he passes on to the authorities. I'm merely trying to make you see it from his point of view. He put forward the suggestion that Tory took the statuette herself and—"

"I never in all my life," Philippa broke in in disgust, "heard such balderdash. You know as well as I do that Tory has told the truth, and I'm certain that Tom knows it, too, so why all this ho-ing and humming and let's-wait-until-we-have-absolute-proof? All I asked him to do was send the statuette back to Lisbon in someone's diplomatic bag. It would have been on its way by now; in fact, it could have arrived—instead of which, here we are sidetracked into building up a case for the police. What did you say to him when he made that silly suggestion?"

"I told him it was impossible for Tory to have done anything of the kind."

"Did you say it calmly, like that?"

"No. With force, because the suggestion made me angry. But you mustn't blame him for trying to get the story straight."

"There's only one angle he didn't bring up. You know that basket Tory left at Austerlitz?"

"Well?"

"If that woman, that Madame Lacoste got—"

"Leblanc."

"If she went back to Austerlitz to get it, she'd find it empty. When Darlan gets in touch with her—which he'll have to do —she'll tell him that it was empty. Do you think he'll believe her?"

"I don't know."

"I wouldn't, in his place. If they're accomplices, he's going to be awfully suspicious when she shows him that basket and tells him there was nothing in it."

"If they're accomplices, she'll have something to say about his having left the booty behind on the train."

"That's right; she will. A nice, friendly meeting it's going to be. Here's my drink. Thank you, Tory." She raised her glass. "Here's to a happy reunion even though it was Dirty Dick Darlan who brought us together. You and I, Tory, could have settled this thing ourselves by this time, if we hadn't been unwilling to involve ourselves with a lot of policemen and reporters. All Lord Tancred has done so far is bring your father here to watch him doing nothing." She looked suspiciously at Edmund. "What's amusing you?"

"I was thinking that you hadn't changed."

"Well, aren't you glad? You liked me as I was."

He laughed, and Tory's eyes rested on him curiously.

"I like you as you are," he said, "but you won't hurry Tancred. He's a man who believes in being thorough."

"I know, I know. But why fetch you all the way to England? I'm glad you're here, but what can you do, after all? You can't catch Darlan; that's what Tom's friends will have to do, if they ever get round to doing it. All I can think of for you to do to fill in time is to take Tory round and show her the sights and try to make up to her for all those years you left her stuck with old aunts and superannuated governesses while you attended to unessentials."

"I'll be happy to take Tory round."

"When my works lets me, I'll come, too. You owe me just as much as you owe Tory." She rose. "And I'm hungry, so let's go and eat. If you were any other man, I'd send you out alone with your daughter, but I'm going along as interpreter—you both need one. Oh, Edmund, I forgot to tell you that you can't fit into this house. I've booked you a room at the hotel my father used to stay at when he came to London. He never found anything to complain about, so it must be all right. You can drop your suitcase there on the way to lunch. Come on, Tory—upstairs to smarten up. Edmund, there's time for you to fix yourself another drink."

The telephone rang as she was halfway up the stairs, and she came down to answer it. When she put down the receiver, she joined Edmund in the sitting room.

"I suppose you gathered who that was?" she asked.

"Yes. Tancred. What did he want?"

"We're all to go to his office this evening."

"Tory, too?"

"Yes, all three of us. Six o'clock."

"Did he have any news?"

"He didn't say. Just the summons. I'm also summoned to dine with him tonight."

"Is that what you assented to with such enthusiasm?"

"Remind me not to be too eager."

He looked at her for a few moments in silence.

"You and he . . . it wouldn't have lasted," he said at last.

"If I'm as good at keeping husbands as I am at keeping fiancés, then you're right: it wouldn't have lasted."

"What exactly went wrong?"

"I wrote and told you."

"Not in detail."

"Well, all he did was take a stand about my going up to Yorkshire to nurse my father. He said, and in a way he was right, that as there was no lack of money, I ought to put my father into the hands of professionals who'd know how to look after him a good deal better than I would. But nursing homes? He walked out of the first one in his pajamas, borrowing on the way out the overcoat of the surgeon who was doing his rounds. I was asked to remove him from the second one because he threw his food out of the window, tray and all. The third one sent him back to me in an ambulance, together with the bills for all the sheets he'd torn up. So he got his way and I went up and nursed him. Tom's attitude never changed; he called it moral blackmail and said I was allowing my father to ruin my life. So helpful. But I missed him when the engagement folded up. I don't think I was ever in love with him—I think I rebounded off you, if you want the truth—but he was more stimulating company than you were. He talked, for one thing. He communicated."

"Hadn't you seen him since then?"

"No. I was two years with my father, and then he died and I sold up and came back to London. By that time Tom was married to someone else. Then there was his divorce, and I wondered whether he'd try to get in touch with me, but he didn't, so I didn't. He'd gone up pretty high by that time; he hadn't got his title, but he was a name. And now we're on dining terms again, which is nice. When he took me out to dinner when we were engaged, people used to say: 'Who's that lovely girl?' Now they'll say: 'Who's Lord Tancred taking out?' It won't be quite the same, but it'll be gratifying to get any kind of attention in the places he goes to."

"Perhaps you'd keep some nights free for me?"

"I might, if it doesn't endanger this delicate new relationship I've got with him. Whether it does or not, I'm glad you're back in my life. I missed you."

"As you missed Tancred?"

"Not at all like that. Quite, quite differently. Are you glad you're here?"

She put the question casually on her way out of the room. He did not reply until she had reached the bend of the staircase. Then he answered quietly.

"Yes," he said. "I'm very glad."

Chapter Seven

When they arrived at Lord Tancred's office, it was in a car that Edmund had rented. They found the office almost empty, but a member of the staff was waiting to escort them to Lord Tancred's room. They found him seated at his desk; in front of it were placed three chairs—armchairs for Philippa and Edmund, a straight-backed chair for Tory.

He rose to greet them; to Philippa and Edmund he was cordial; to Tory he meant to be, but the sight of her made him feel, as he had felt on their first meeting, that, for a child round whom was gathering so much of importance, she was showing remarkably little emotion. Whether she was hiding anything or not, he decided that her self-control was uncanny. Certainly it was irritating; he had already gone to great trouble on her behalf, and he felt that he merited more from her than a polite, murmured greeting.

He seated himself and drew forward a file in which were a few sheets of paper. Before he could speak, Philippa addressed him.

"On our way here just now," she said, "Edmund raised a point about expenses—the expense of instituting inquiries. He—"

"I said," Edmund interrupted, "that I would like to meet any expenses incurred in the course of the investigation."

"And what I told him," Philippa resumed, "was that any investigations conducted at the level at which you're conducting them are always charged to the taxpayer. Isn't that right?"

"If it's right, it's wrong," Edmund said. "But I'm more worried about the trouble we're giving you than the expense. Have you found out anything?"

"Not much," Lord Tancred answered. "As I explained to you, I could put forward no proof that there had been a theft, and that hampered my inquiries. But I have done a good deal of telephoning across the Channel during the past few hours, and certain facts have come to light."

"Such as what?" Philippa asked.

"It is established that on the ninth of January an Englishman who was travelling from Hendaye to Paris left the train at Bayonne. He ran after a porter and said that his luggage had been placed by mistake on the wagon that the porter was wheeling. In fact, his luggage was not on it. It was not anywhere on Bayonne station, and officials made it clear to the Englishman that no disembarking passengers, with or without two suitcases and a golf bag, had passed through the ticket barrier at the exit. The Englishman took the afternoon train to Paris."

"So there's a clear corroboration of Tory's story," said Philippa. "Anything else?"

"Yes. When the train on which the Englishman had been travelling—the train in which he and Tory travelled from Hendaye to Bayonne—arrived in Paris, two suitcases and a golf bag were found on the luggage rack of one of the compartments. The luggage was claimed that same evening by the owner, who gave his name as Mr. Darlan, with an address in London. There is also some news relating to the basket which Tory left at Austerlitz. This was claimed on the evening of the ninth by a Frenchwoman who gave her name as Madame Marchand; she explained that she had left it in the cloakroom earlier in the day. That was all the attendant required to know, since the basket was empty and was of no value, and worth nothing to anyone but its owner. But as Madame Marchand was leaving, one of those incidents occurred which you can put down as coincidence, or fate, or simply bad luck for Madame Marchand: A woman coming in greeted her at the door, and the attendant was alert enough to notice that she addressed her by another name. She questioned the woman, who said that the attendant must have made a mistake; the woman who had just left was not called Madame Marchand; her name was Madame Leblanc and she was the owner of a shop in the Rue Oriel. There could be no mistake; she knew the shop and she knew Madame Leblanc well. Inquiries are now being made about Madame Leblanc; we shall have to wait and see where they lead. And that is all I have to tell you—except one rather damning fact: that the address given by Mr. Darlan has been found to be false. The street in London does not exist."

Philippa drew a deep breath.

"A fine pair," she said.

"It seems so." Lord Tancred spoke dryly. "If Tory had reported the circumstances to you immediately on her arrival in London, and if you had come to me at once, there would have been more hope of getting results."

"But she didn't, and I didn't, and we're both very sorry, but you know now that Tory's reporting was accurate, so will you send that saint back to Lisbon?"

He did not reply; his eyes were on Tory.

"Can you offer any explanation," he asked her, "as to why, if Mr. Darlan's luggage was found on the rack of a compartment which, as far as can be gathered, was in the same coach as that in which you and he were seated, neither you nor he saw it?"

She answered with composure.

"It wasn't there when he looked."

"You said that you gave the shirt, the shirt in which the statuette was wrapped, to a Portuguese immigrant on the train. When?"

"It was about twelve o'clock, just after the attendant had walked along the corridor with tickets for lunch. It was before going to join the Portuguese that I found what was in the basket."

"You hadn't looked inside it before—for instance, when Mr. Darlan was out of the train getting something for his headache?"

"No. He told me not to touch it, because he'd wrapped a bottle of shaving lotion in it and he didn't want it to get broken."

"You believed what he said?"

"Yes."

"Having joined the Portuguese, you stayed with them?"

"Yes. I stayed in their compartment until we got to Paris."

"Will you tell me once again, please, exactly how you spent your time when Mr. Darlan left the train the first time?"

"I walked to the end of the corridor and stood there watching the Cruzons' luggage being put on the wagon, and I watched the Portuguese at the other end of the platform, and then I went back to the compartment and stood with my back to it watching a train on the other side of the station. Then Mr. Darlan came back and looked in and said his luggage wasn't there."

There was a pause.

"Will you assure me—" Lord Tancred spoke in a slow and grave tone. "Will you assure all of us here that this—which is the very crux of the matter—is absolutely true: that Mr. Darlan returned to the train, looked up on the luggage rack and discovered that his luggage was not on it?"

"Yes."

"Would you be prepared to swear to that?"

"Yes." Her voice and attitude were alike calm. "Yes, I would. There was nothing of his there. Only my own things."

"I can't understand," Philippa said in a puzzled tone, "why you keep going back to that. Why should Tory have to swear that the luggage wasn't there? If it had been there, why would this Darlan have leapt off the train again and gone chasing a porter?"

"Why indeed? But I return to that point of the story," Lord Tancred told her, "because it is the only part which I still find it impossible to accept. It is obvious that Tory is both observant and intelligent; could she stand in the doorway of a compartment, even though her back is turned to it, while someone enters and removes two large suitcases and a golf bag? The window is open, but it is not conceivable that anybody would climb in from the station, in full view of officials and bystanders, and remove some luggage; if they had done this during the time Tory was standing at the exit door, she would have been able to hear or to see what was going on. So we have to conclude that someone entered the compartment and removed the luggage while Tory was standing at the exit door and looking out onto the platform to watch the Cruzons and the Portuguese. Anybody doing this would have had to take it away in the direction opposite to that in which Tory would return to the compartment—the direction which Tory later took on her way to the third-class compartments. How could anybody have hoped to conceal two large suitcases and a golf bag? The owner, if he had gone in search of them and looked into every compartment, would certainly have found them without difficulty. So it seems to me that there is a missing factor, something which has slipped Tory's mind or which she is keeping to herself."

Tory, under scrutiny from three pairs of eyes, remained unmoved. She was looking at Lord Tancred, and although the others found it difficult to interpret the look, it was certainly not one of doubt or distress. Her thoughts at that moment were in fact almost wholly admiring. It was very clever of him, she felt, to have put his finger right on the very spot. He might still be groping, but he was groping in the right place, and if she hadn't told the truth, if she hadn't been able to feel secure because the truth was the same however many times you told it, he would undoubtedly have been able to probe and probe until he found out everything he wanted to know. She had not liked him at their first meeting; she liked him less and less, but she admitted to herself that he was clever.

He spoke with resignation.

"So we are forced to accept the fact that two suitcases and a golf bag, having been spirited away from their place on the rack in Mr. Darlan's compartment, were replaced before the end of the journey."

"Somebody could have been looking for something inside them, couldn't they?" Philippa suggested. "Look how terrified he got when he found them missing."

"I doubt if anything in his luggage was as valuable as the statuette which he left behind in an open basket, covered by a shirt and disguised as shaving lotion." Lord Tancred picked up the papers and replaced them in the file. "That's all I have to tell you," he said.

"All? It's enough, isn't it?" Edmund spoke in surprise. "They're on the track of two thieves."

"I hope so. I was asked whether I could furnish any information about Darlan's movements in Portugal. Perhaps you know something about this?"

"I don't know very much. He came out from England at about the same time every year, installed himself in his Estoril hotel and played golf. He used to go into Lisbon now and then, and he took trips up north. His only interest from the sight-seeing point of view seemed to be churches—and one can now see why."

Lord Tancred had risen.

"Philippa is dining with me. Can I offer you a car to take Tory and yourself back?" he asked Edmund.

"No, thanks. I got myself one of those rented cars this afternoon. Thanks for all you've done about this business."

He took Tory away, and Philippa waited a few minutes for Lord Tancred to clear his desk. Then she went down with him to the street, where his car was waiting. He dismissed the chauffeur and took the wheel. As he and Philippa drove away, there was a slight frown on her face.

"I'm puzzled," she said. "You don't like her, do you?"

"You're referring to Tory?"

"Of course I'm referring to Tory. Why don't you like her?"

"I haven't said I—"

"Do you or don't you?"

"I don't really like any children—you should know that by now."

"This isn't any children. This is more personal. You've got it in for her."

"Don't talk nonsense. My only feeling is that she isn't frank."

"You mean she's a liar?"

"No, I don't. It would be easier for me if she were. You can trip up juvenile liars, as a rule. You can get them to contradict themselves. You can get through the screen they're putting up and find your way to the full facts. But this child—you were right in regarding her as adult—has a self-command I've never encountered in anybody of her age."

"You're annoyed because she stood up to your cross-examination. She's a nice child."

"If you say so."

"But, as you've just admitted, she's adult. From the moment I met her, I've had the feeling that we were on equal terms. She may be quiet, but she's not mousy. She doesn't say much until you've pulled the right switch. She isn't wrapped up in herself, as most children seem to me to be; she's interested in other people and other people's affairs. If you knew more about her, you'd feel sorry for her for having been surrounded for ten years by all those old women."

"Why sorry for her?"

"Use your imagination. It must have been like growing up in Queen Victoria's day: cooks working in a vast basement, food sent up on pulleys and meals going on all day long, one old aunt ringing for beef soup while the other demands chicken cutlets, and all the servants rounded up to go to Mass in the chapel, and antiquated hot-water systems and a special dining room for the priests and the nuns who drop in to conduct services or pray for the poor."

"But all this—"

"And every Sunday, the old aunts sitting at a table in the hall doling out pensions, following a tradition instituted by some ancestor a couple of centuries ago."

"I really don't see—"

"From what I can make out, the house is as solid as the Tower of London, and life inside its walls hasn't changed since Lisbon picked itself up after the great earthquake, if you know when that was."

"Do you?"

"Yes, I do. Seventeen something. The point of what I've been saying—"

"Ah. The point."

"—is that Tory has practically had to bring herself up. In all that household, from cooks to clerics, she hasn't had, as far as I can make out, a single soul to talk to, really *talk* to. So all her life she grew up taking in a lot and giving out practically nothing, and that's what's made her the way she is; that and the fact that she takes after her father, who isn't exactly inarticulate but who keeps his thoughts and his reactions to himself. If her father—"

"Ah."

"Will you stop saying 'Ah' all the time I'm talking? I was saying that if her father had been a talkative type, she might have inherited more self-expression. But if Edmund feels anything deeply, he goes dumb. He'll talk freely about facts; if you work at it, you can even manage to drag opinions out of him. But what he's feeling . . . never."

"Yet he once made you understand that he was in love with you."

"Only with my assistance. I managed to pin him down to a concrete proposal of marriage just forty-eight hours before he took off on that fatal, or would it be fateful, trip to Macau. As I told you long ago, there wasn't even time to buy me a ring, so I had to wait until I was engaged to you and you provided one—a lovely, expensive one. Given the same set of circumstances today, I'd keep it and take it to the nearest jeweler and see what I could get for it. I always regretted giving it back after we had our farewell fight. Did you use it for your next fiancée?"

"No."

"Why not?"

"I thought of it, I still think of it as your ring."

She turned to gaze at him, her eyes wide.

"You don't mean you've still got it?"

"Yes."

"Why on *earth?*"

He hesitated, his eyes on the road, his profile revealing nothing.

"Because I never succeeded in making up my mind," he said at last, "whether I'd acted rightly or wrongly."

"Wrongly. I told you so at the time. I told you you were mean and self-opinionated and—"

"Shall we review the circumstances?"

"If you're looking for excuses, reviewing won't help you."

"It may help you to see the matter in its proper light."

"Then go ahead and review."

"The choice was not mine but yours: a choice between marrying me or going up to Yorkshire, for a period which nobody could have assessed, to nurse your father. You chose to go. When I told you just now that I'd never been able to make up my mind whether I was right or wrong, I meant right or wrong in not waiting to see how things turned out. You might have been induced to leave him, in time. He might have died in a short while—which in fact he did."

"You knew at the time that no nursing home would keep him. When did this remorse begin to bite you?"

"I think that my marriage, so soon after we brought our engagement to an end, was an unconscious attempt to—"

"What went wrong with it?"

"I did."

"You can't mean that you, the all-but-virgin tycoon, went off the rails?"

"No. My wife and I weren't suited, but it might have worked out if I hadn't spent so much of my time at the office. I left her to amuse herself."

"And she did?"

"She did. I never blamed her."

"No, you only divorced her. You've never asked me how I got into the china business."

"How did you get into the china business?"

"I suppose you could call it chance. It was through the last nurse who came to help me look after my father. She was in a state of dither because her brother had asked her to give up nursing and join him. He was opening a china shop in London, and there were to have been three of them: the brother, another sister and the sister's husband. But then the sister decided to leave her husband, so that left two, and this nurse was to have been the third—only she didn't want to give up nursing. When my father died and she left, she was still thinking it over. Then I sold the house and came back to London and bought the house I'm in now, and started to think about getting myself a job. I'd inherited my father's money, so I felt it needn't be a full-time job. I'd made up my mind to look up the agency I used to know, and—"

"The agency that sent you to work for me?"

"The same. I'll wait while you say what you have to say."

"They grossly overstated your capabilities."

"Yes, they did. I hoped they'd overstate them again. I was actually—this part you'll find hard to believe—I was actually in the bus on my way to the agency when I saw a sign being put up near the milk bar I always go to. I recognized the name—the nurse's name—and felt curious to know whether she had decided to join the business, so at the next stop I got off the bus and went back to find out. I found she'd decided to stick to nursing, so her brother and her separated-from-husband sister were still looking for a third. And so, skipping all the dull bits like deciding to go into partnership and getting advice from my lawyer and my banker and so on—I was in the china business."

"Typical."

"Typical of what?"

"Typical of your usual headstrong action. Is it successful?"

"Too successful. So successful that the brother, Douglas by name, is planning to buy up the next-door premises. But he'll have to look for two new partners, because the sister's going back to her husband, and I've decided to get out."

"You're tired of being a successful businesswoman?"

"I could go along with the business angle; it's the personal angle that made me decide I'd had enough."

"Ah. The brother."

"Ah. There you go again."

"He has too warm an admiration for your business capabilities?"

"You could put it that way. Before you say 'Ah' again, isn't it odd that this is the first time you and Edmund and I have, as it were, come together? First there was Edmund and myself; then there was you and myself, but never before the three of us happily united. The past—by which I mean those two engagements—doesn't seem to have left much impression. Looking back on ours, I've often thought that I agreed to marry you because I'd never really got over Edmund's shall-we-call-it-defection. Why you wanted to marry me I've never been able to decide."

He spoke deliberately.

"For reasons which were not too clear at the time, but which became clearer when you walked into my office the other day, and which have been getting clearer ever since."

There was a pause before she spoke.

"A compliment?" she asked.

"No. An admission of failure. Failure to understand, years ago, that my chief motive in marrying was to restore my lost self-respect. Not once, during that struggle between us, did I believe that you would win and I would lose. Everything had always gone as I'd wanted it—until then. God knows I'd worked hard enough for success—but I'd achieved it. I was less than forty, and I'd managed to get everything I'd gone after. Then I came up against something I wasn't equipped to deal with: the feminine mind, class three-C. I could have dealt with a clever woman; she would have been able to follow my arguments. I couldn't deal with a woman whose brain was buried deep under layers of sentiment, impulse and obstinacy."

"Meaning me?"

"Meaning you. I'm not surprised you have a fellow-feeling for this child of Edmund Brooke's. I thought at first that it was pure sentiment—that is, the fact that she was his child. But it's not that. It's a fellow-feeling because you're both, she and you, in your different ways, impossible to pin down. You must have been corresponding with him pretty regularly for him to have asked you to act as her guardian in England."

"Regularly is right. Two lines every Christmas—that is, two from me to him, and the same from him to me. But when he wrote last September, it was more than two lines; it was a whole letter, all about Tory and his decision to send her to England."

"Didn't he ever suggest your visiting Lisbon?"

"No. Which is why I didn't go. What are you stopping for?"

"Because this is the restaurant in which we're going to dine."

"We haven't taken long to get to it. You always used to go a long way round when you took me out."

"I shall take you a long way round on the way home."

He left the car to be parked by an employee, and followed her inside.

When they returned to Elcombe Grove, there was a light showing in the window of Philippa's sitting room.

"Edmund's still here. Coming in?" she asked.

"No."

He drove away, and she let herself into the house. Edmund, getting up lazily from the chair in which he had been dozing, yawned and stretched.

"Good morning," he greeted her. "Did you have a pleasant night?"

"Yes, thank you. Did Tory go to bed early?"

"Fairly. We went out to supper. Not a protracted meal, like the one you had; just a simple supper, and straight home after it."

"Did you eat at the milk bar?"

"God forbid. Could I help myself to a drink—one for the road?"

"Of course. Help me to one, too. The same nightcap as the one you used to pour out for me eleven . . . or was it twelve years ago?"

"Almost twelve. What did you and Tancred talk about?"

"The past." She had settled herself on the sofa; she held out her hand to take the drink he brought her. "We also glanced at the present. He still thinks that Tory's holding something back. Tom's like that; if he gets an idea, it sticks."

He was back in the deep chair, his legs outstretched. He spoke thoughtfully.

"What surprises me is the way she seems to have shelved the affair. As far as I can see, she's put it right out of her mind. She must know that what Tancred's doing is being done chiefly for her, to save her from further involvement, but far from appearing interested, not to mention grateful, she made not one reference to the affair once we'd left his office."

"She didn't like Darlan. I don't think she cares what happens to him."

"What makes you say she didn't like him? Did she tell you so?"

"No. But you can sense it. He used her and her basket for his unlawful purposes, and that's enough to have made her loathe him. Will you go home? I'm sleepy and I've got to get up for work tomorrow."

"Today. Will you have lunch with Tory and me?"

"I'm sorry, I can't. I've got to have lunch with my two partners, who soon won't be my partners anymore. It won't be a happy lunch, but it's time we got the breakup settled."

"Why does there have to be a breakup?"

"One partner's going back to her husband and the other—her brother—wants to turn the business from a nice, family affair into a big-business concern. Which I don't want. He also wants to marry me, and I don't seem to be able to find any way of convincing him that I'm not interested, so the only thing to do is get out."

"You should marry."

"I should. Third time lucky—perhaps. If you're going to switch that lunch invitation to a dinner one, don't because I've promised to dine with Tom."

"Again?"

"I can hardly refuse, can I, when he's going to so much trouble for us all? Besides, I like going out with him. Tonight, everybody recognized him the moment he walked in, and as he's the most eligible bachelor, sorry, divorcé in town, I came in for a lot of attention, too." She emptied her glass and looked across at him. "Edmund, this'll make you angry, but I'm going to say it: Why haven't you ever spoken to Tory about her mother?"

He had risen to take her glass. He stood very still, turning it slowly round and round in his hands.

"I couldn't," he said at last.

"It was her *right.*"

"I know. But I couldn't."

"She knows nothing about the past, except what she's picked up from listening to the old aunts and that Frenchwoman who seems to have acted as a bodyguard. Even if you didn't think it worth while telling her that you and I were once engaged, you could have told her something about her mother's family, her mother's Macau background. She grew up knowing that she mustn't mention her mother to you. How could you do that to her?"

"Self-protection. A selfish desire on my part to avoid constant reminders."

"But it's just that that I can't understand. You loved your wife and you were given great happiness; not for long, but at least you had it. All your memories of her, except the very last, must be happy ones. When people die, we can keep them in our minds, even in a way in our lives. Tory could have grown up with all your happy memories of her mother—where you met, how you met, how you fell in love and married. She had a right to know."

"Yes. All right. You've said it."

"I'm sorry. No, I'm not. It had to be said."

"I'm not making excuses, but . . . you don't know Tory's aunts and you don't know the kind of atmosphere I went back to after Vitorina died. I had three choices: to mourn in their way, which just stopped short of wailing and breast-beating; to permit constant references and reminders in the form of Masses, prayers, condolences and tearful sympathy; or—the third choice—to shut it all away and put an end to it. I put an end to it."

"I see."

"I don't think you do. In this country, the kind of excessive mourning that the Victorians went in for has gone out of fashion. No more black horses with nodding plumes, no more retreating from the world or going into a decline. But there are still places in which there are old aunts who believe that a show of grief is the only way of showing that you're grieving. If you follow me."

She rose, took the glass from him, put it on the table and drew his arms round her.

"I follow you. I can always follow you if you give me something to follow, if you communicate. Anytime you want to communicate, there's a hot line you could use—if you wanted to. If you never use it, it might get disconnected; hasn't that occurred to you?"

"Yes."

"Then act on it. And now kiss me good night."

"Not good night. Good morning. Did Tancred kiss you good night, good morning?"

She made an impatient sound.

"Oh Edmund, of *course* he did. See if you can do it better."

Chapter Eight

Before Philippa left for work a few hours later, there was a ring at the front door. Tory was up but not yet dressed, and was wearing one of Philippa's jackets as a dressing gown. Philippa went into the hall and on opening the front door found Edmund on the doorstep, huddled in an overcoat but hatless, his hair ruffled by the strong, bitterly cold wind. He came in hastily and closed the door behind him.

"Brrr! What weather!" he shivered. "They could put penguins in the parks." Without removing his overcoat, he followed her into the kitchen, said good morning to Tory and demanded hot coffee.

"What got you up at this hour?" Philippa asked him.

"The cold. Next time you book a room for me, make sure it has a heating system."

"My father—"

"—was a hardy Yorkshireman, who probably turned off the radiators and threw open the window just to make himself feel at home." He intercepted a slice of buttered toast on its way from Tory to Philippa, and bit into it. "Hurry up with that coffee."

"Why don't you buy yourself a real winter overcoat?" Philippa asked him. "That one you've got on was built for light summer breezes."

"I know. I thought I'd drive you to work, wait till the Banks open, get myself some money and then invest in some long woollen combinations. I wish to God I'd brought my warm sweaters—but I wasn't given enough time to remember what sort of climate I was coming to. All the time I was packing, the consular car purred outside. Any more toast, Tory?"

"Yes. I'm buttering it for you."

"Thanks. Want to come shopping with me?"

To his surprise, she hesitated. Seeing the astonishment on his face, Philippa laughed.

"Tory's made friends with a dog," she explained. "You're going to meet him, Tory—isn't that right?"

"I don't have to go," Tory said, "but he'll only be here for a few more days, so I'd like to play with him."

"Play where?" her father asked. "Is there a local park?"

"No. There's a piece of waste ground behind the house," Philippa told him. "Open to all."

"I see. Well, when I've done my shopping, I'll come back here and sit and read the paper until you've finished playing with the dog," he said to Tory. "Don't be too late."

"No, I won't. Will you be lunching with us?" she asked Philippa.

"No, I can't. I'd much rather be with you and your father, but I'll come straight back here after lunch and we'll think of something to do in the afternoon. Edmund, you haven't time for another cup of coffee; I've got to go."

When Tory reached the waste ground, there was no sign of Derek or Leo. After waiting for a time, she began to walk in the direction of Colony Street. When she reached it, she discovered the reason for Derek's failure to appear: A van had run into the back of a car, which had been pushed sideways into the path of an oncoming taxi. There were no casualties, but there was a large crowd; two policemen were attempting to restore order, and there were noisy recriminations and a spirited fistfight. From the top step of the nearest house, Derek was enjoying an unimpeded view.

Tory turned away and walked down the steps to Mrs. Tesworth's rooms. She found Mrs. Tesworth seated in her chair, placidly knitting, unwashed tea cups on a table close by.

"Sit down, Tory, ducks," she invited. "You won't get young Derek away, not yet. Was 'e holding Leo on 'is lead?"

"Yes."

"Then that's all right. Don't like to think of that dog runnin' loose. I made a nice cuppa just now; if you'd like some, it's still 'ot."

"No, thank you."

"Was Mr. Barlow up there in the street?"

"No."

"Then I 'ope 'e'll stay 'ome. This kind of weather does for 'im, gets right down into 'is lungs and plays 'im up. But he goes out once a day, all the year round, frost or snow; says 'e couldn't stand bein' cooped up all day, like me. Funny when you come to think of it: when we was young, I thought I'd be the one to take care of 'im when we was old, but that isn't 'ow it's turned out. It's not 'im that's the crock, it's me. 'E's good to me, really good. Not a day passes but 'e's knockin' on that door, just to know if I'm all right. It's not many men you'd find who'd go to that trouble for an old has-been like me. But 'e's a good man. Good all the way through."

Tory was wondering why there had never been any mention, in all Mrs. Tesworth's monologues, of Mr. Tesworth. She had asked Derek if he knew anything about him, and had found that he had never heard Mrs. Tesworth mention his name. She had learned so much of the picturesque Tesworth past that it seemed a pity not to be able to find a place among the colourful details for a key figure like a husband. While Mrs. Tesworth described an adventure on a long-past, rainy Bank Holiday, she sat trying to decide in what form she could put a question. A direct approach seemed indelicate. She chose something more oblique, and waited until there was a pause long enough to voice it.

"Did Mr. Tesworth die a long time ago?"

The knitting fell slowly onto Mrs. Tesworth's lap. She turned her head and for the space of fifteen seconds stared at Tory with her mouth open.

" 'Oo did you say?" she inquired at last in a dazed voice.

The blank astonishment was daunting, but Tory persevered.

"Mr. Tesworth. Your husband. Did he . . . did he die?"

"Whatever made you ask that?" Mrs. Tesworth asked in the same tone of astonishment.

"I just . . . I just wondered, that's all."

"Fancy you coming out with that! It gave me a turn, 'earing you say the name. I 'aven't 'eard it mentioned, not for forty years and more. Whatever made you think of 'im?"

"I was interested in a lot of the things you told me, but you never said anything about him, and—"

"Interested. That's what I can't get over. Interested. You're not just sayin' that; you mean it. That's what made me go on talkin', feelin' there was someone interested in them old days. You're the first kid I ever come across who could sit and listen to anything but the telly. If you want the truth, you don't strike me as bein' a kid. Many a time, talkin', I've found myself tellin' you somethin' I wouldn't 'ave thought it right to tell any ordinary kid. I'm sorry you're goin' away."

"I'll be back when the Easter holidays start. I'd like to see you then."

"An' I'd like to see you. With Derek gone, 'ow d'you think I'm goin' to feel? Derek and 'is dog, both of 'em goin'. There won't be any liveliness anymore. But you'll forget all about old Mrs. T. when you get to school."

"No, I won't. Did Mr. Tesworth—"

"There you go again." Mrs. Tesworth, who had resumed her knitting, put it down once more on her lap. "Which one d'you want to know about?"

"Which one?"

"There was two."

"You mean two husbands?"

"I mean two Mr. Tesworths."

"Oh. You mean . . . "

"It's not out of the way, 'aving two husbands of the same name. The only out-of-the-way thing was that I was married to 'em both at the same time."

"The . . . "

"They didn't know it, and I didn't know it. I married Bob Tesworth when I was about sixteen, or maybe seventeen; I'm not sure which, but I know it was a silly stage, and even when I was coming out o' church on 'is arm I wondered what I'd done it for. They said it was because 'e was going off to the war, but it wasn't that; it was just that I was too excitable, and never knew me own mind from one day to the next. Well, we had two 'ole weeks as man an' wife, and then 'e went to the front and I got a telegram to say I was a widder. Then, next, I married 'is brother Mervyn. An' 'e went to war, same's as 'is brother'd done, and 'e was killed, same's as 'is brother'd been, but it came out that Bob hadn't been killed at all, 'e'd only been wounded bad and taken prisoner. An' 'e died in the end, an' when I'd been told, and I'd 'ad time to sit down and work it out, I found I'd been Mrs. Bob and Mrs. Mervyn at the same time. You'd think that'd make me remember 'em, but to tell you the truth, if you put a snap of 'em both down in front of me now and said 'Guess who?' I'd 'ave to stop and think. You 'ave to be married proper, I mean married for longer than a month or two, before it leaves a mark. I never felt properly married, and I never felt a widder. There were no other Tesworths anywhere around to remind me, and I was busy workin' 'ard, and nobody ever seemed to remember what 'appened to my husband, and I never let on there'd been two at once, and so it all died, as you might say, a natural death. Even Derek's mum, when she came 'ere, she never remembered a word about any Tesworths, although I could've told 'er if she'd asked me, only she didn't, that she was related to some Tesworths on 'er mother's side. Mad to get married again, she was. Me, I thought two was enough, and there was Mr. Barlow; I couldn't 'ave left 'im. So you see what a turn you give me when you came out with Mr. Tesworth's name."

"Did Mr. Barlow ever get married?"

"No, ducks. He's not the sort that gets married. I looked after 'im for years, but, like I said, it's 'im as looks after me now. If you want to go and play with Leo, you'll find 'em ready to go now; you can see the crowd's going away."

But although she caught up with Derek and Leo, there was no time to play; her father was waiting for her. She found him reading the newspaper in the sitting room.

"I've booked a table for lunch," he told her. "Old coaching inn. How long will it take you to get ready?"

"I'm ready now."

As they drove out of London, she felt that conversation was not called for; she looked out of her window, and sometimes at the map her father had given her to enable her to follow the route. She had an idea, vague as yet, that silences between herself and him might in time lose their awkwardness and become restful silences, during which she could think her own thoughts without worrying about suitable subjects to discuss.

But when they were seated at their table, in a room in which oak and leather and sporting prints predominated, she found that there were to be no awkward silences. Her father emerged from behind a large menu to make suggestions for her meal, allowed her to make the final choice and then relinquished the menu to the waiter and leaned back to study her. Soon he put a question.

"Have you decided what you think of Philippa?"

For once, she was caught off guard; her eyes, meeting his across the table, told him plainly what she thought of Philippa. Then she answered quietly.

"I like her very much."

"And she likes you. Which means that you'll enjoy staying with her at the beginning and end of your school terms. We're lucky to have a relation in central London. There are Brookes up and down the country, but I've lost touch with them all. Have you written to your aunts in Portugal?"

"No. I thought ... I didn't know what to say about Saint Christopher."

"Don't say anything. You should write to them, but without any mention of what's happened. When we've got something definite to tell them, we'll tell them." He paused. "I suppose I don't have to tell you that I'm sorry I took Mr. Darlan on trust? Philippa blames me, but I didn't feel at the time that there was any need to go to the lengths of screening a man merely because he was going to travel on the same train as my daughter. She thinks my suspicions should have been aroused, but doesn't say what should have aroused them. When did she tell you that she and I had once been engaged?"

"When we got to the house after she'd met me at the station. I saw your photograph on her dressing table."

He stared at her, astonishment on his face.

"My photograph?"

"Yes. She keeps it there. And the bear."

"What bear?"

"The koala bear you won at a fair. She told me then."

"She says I should have told you before. Perhaps she's right. But—this isn't an excuse, it's merely a comment—all these things seemed very long ago and far away when you and I were in Lisbon. Coming to England, meeting Philippa again, seeing and hearing her, brought it all back."

"I'm glad you . . . "

"You're glad I what?"

"Went on writing to her . . . afterwards."

"You could hardly call it writing. But we kept in touch. It was she who began our correspondence, and I'm grateful to her. She never sent me much news of herself, but we've got to thank her for writing at all. We've got to thank her for a lot of other things, too."

He was silent for some time, staring absently at the tablecloth. His forefinger found and captured a crumb that had fallen from the basket of bread rolls; he took it on a slow journey round his plate.

"Did she talk to you much about your mother?" he asked, without looking up.

"No, not much. She said she didn't know my mother. She only knew people who'd met her and who told her about her."

He raised his eyes to her face.

"You look like her," he said. "At least, she must have looked exactly like you when she was ten. I didn't meet her until she was seventeen. I was just over thirty. If you've ever read stories about people falling in love the instant they set eyes on one another . . . well, that happened to us. After we met, we thought it strange, even extraordinary that I'd been to Macau so often and left again without any feeling of her presence there. Perhaps you think that's silly."

"No, I don't."

"Although she was so young when we married, she wasn't immature. In that, too, you're like her; I've always thought that you were very grown-up for your age. She—"

To her bitter disappointment, he was interrupted. Their food was being served. The wine list was brought and he studied it; he asked her what she would like to drink. But to her relief, when these matters were attended to, he did not begin to eat; he sat looking absently at his food.

"Go on talking," she begged.

He did not seem to have heard her, but he went on.

"She was living with her father's relations, in a house that had once been very luxurious—but when I saw it, it was in great need of repair and the furniture inside it was very shabby. Your grandmother, Margarida, sister of Pilar and Piedade, had married a man who had a lot of money and a successful business, but by the time he and Margarida died the money had gone and the business was doing badly. Opinion in Macau was divided about whose fault it was. Some people said that Margarida had ruined her husband by trying to turn his house into another Casa Fenix and living in the style in which she had been brought up. Other people thought that her husband was the one who had done the spending. For myself, I was glad that there wasn't much money, because if the family had still been rich, I think they would have made more fuss about your mother marrying me. As it was, the only objection they raised was that I was a non-Catholic. But we were married two months after we met, and I took your mother to Lisbon, where . . . Tory, you're not eating."

"I will in a minute. Please go on."

"We had decided that Lisbon was the place in which we would like to live. You were born at the Casa Fenix and your mother and I left you in the care of your great-aunts while we came on a visit to England—I wanted to take her round to all my relations and show her to them. The first visit was to be to Philippa and her father in Yorkshire. We were on our way there when the car in which we were driving . . . Your mother was killed in the accident. I was unhurt. There seemed no point in taking you away from the care of people who loved you and who were your relations and who would look after you when I was away. They thought it was unwise of me to go on looking for a house of my own, and suggested my living at the Casa Fenix. I agreed—rightly or wrongly. Rightly or wrongly, I left your well-being in their hands. I didn't interfere—except when it seemed to me that you were getting too much chapel, too many priests, too many prayers, so I took you to a Protestant church to restore some kind of balance. You enjoyed singing the Protestant hymns." He picked up his fork. "I told you before you came to England that you would be able to choose, in due course, which country you'd rather live in—England or Portugal. You've got a two-way choice in religion, too; you can be Catholic like your mother or Protestant like me, and either way will be all right in the long run. Tory, eat; you're letting your food get cold."

She began to eat. He had hardly expected her to comment on what he had been saying, but he would have liked to be able to guess what she was thinking. Were all children as inscrutable as this one sitting on the other side of the table? Were they all as secretive? Or had he failed to find a key that would open the way to confidence? Was she going to grow up like himself, was she going to find it impossible to express what she was feeling? Would she always be self-contained, giving nothing away?

What was she like, this child of his? She was affectionate—she loved Philippa. She had humour; it was seldom seen, but it was there. She had brains and knew how to use them. How could he get to know her? Philippa, who had known her for less than a week, had succeeded in getting closer to her than anybody else had ever done.

He spoke on trivial subjects until they had finished their meal and coffee had been placed before him. He pushed the coffeepot across to Tory, and she understood that he wished her to pour it out for him.

"I've been thinking about your future," he said. "Our future. Would you like to live in a house of our own in Lisbon? Or near Lisbon?"

She handed him his coffee and then sat trying to decide how much he had meant by the words—the first suggestion he had ever made of a home apart from the Casa Fenix. How could he have a home if he was never in it? What about his work, his travel? The possibility, introduced so suddenly into the conversation, threw her mind into confusion. She would have liked to leave the table, leave the restaurant and find a quiet place in which she could be alone and let her imagination roam. A home of their own, without the supervising aunts, without the ever-present Mademoiselle Barrault, a home without vast, empty, echoing rooms. A house without a daily procession of pensioners, priests, nuns. Just themselves—and a Leo of their own.

She heard her father speaking again.

"You're wondering," he said, "whether that was a suggestion or a vague possibility. It was more. It was a definite decision. I have to go back to South America when Lord Tancred has cleared up this Darlan matter—but it's the last time I'll go. Retirement isn't what's in my mind. I'm too young to retire. All I mean to do is hand over the mobile part of the job to someone else, and take over the Lisbon office. I won't change my mind. The decision stands. So if you feel that the idea of having a home of our own is a good one, you'll have to study the problem of where we live from the angle of commuting—that's to say, the house would have to be somewhere which would allow me to get to work in Lisbon five days a week, and back again, without wasting too many hours. First of all, do you think the idea is a good one, or do you feel that, having lived for so long with your aunts, you don't want to leave them?"

She hesitated. "Aunt Pilar and Aunt Piedade wouldn't mind. And Jesuina wouldn't know. I'd have to go and visit Aunt Pilar and Aunt Piedade, but as long as I did that, they wouldn't mind. They'd say they did, but I don't think they'd really mind."

"Well then. Any ideas about a house?"

To his amazement, the answer came unhesitatingly.

"Yes. Could we live at the Quinta do Rio?"

He was too surprised to speak. She smiled, waiting until he had recovered.

"What in the world made you suggest the Quinta do Rio?" he asked at last. "I didn't think you'd ever heard of it."

"Aunt Pilar had to go there once, when I was little. She took me. You went and saw it once, didn't you?"

Her last words were an acknowledgment of a change in their relationship; she would not have spoken them if he had not spoken to her of her mother.

"Yes, I went there with your mother," he answered. "The house belonged to Margarida, and your mother and I went to look at it when we were looking for a place to live. Margarida left it to Pilar."

"Did my mother like it?"

"Yes, she did—very much. But the question of commuting came up then, as it'll have to come up now. We decided that it was too far out."

"When you took her to see it, there was no bridge across the river. Now there is."

"True."

"It's near Setubal, and from Setubal it isn't far into Lisbon. That wouldn't be too long, would it?"

"No. How much do you remember of the house? As I remember it, it was pretty derelict."

She closed her eyes, and she was standing in a flagged courtyard that had a three-way view; she could see the front of the beautiful old house, and the tangle of orchard, and the stretch of river beyond, with little white sails appearing and disappearing among the branches of the trees that lined the bank. She opened her eyes and spoke.

"A nice big hall," she said slowly. "You go in through a big door—a double door. Inside, there's a double staircase and a sort of gallery at the top, and you walk along the gallery to get to the bedrooms. There's a lovely big drawing room, and a dining room with a terrace outside, and then you go through to the kitchen—"

She stopped abruptly, remembering the kitchen.

"Go on. The kitchen?"

"I suppose," she admitted reluctantly, "it's what you said: derelict. Why did they let it get like that?"

"There was no 'they' to stop the rot. The house hadn't been lived in for years. Margarida was in Macau and nobody else seemed to want the house. When she left it to Pilar, Pilar put it on the market."

"But nobody bought it. Couldn't you pay to have it repaired? You could buy it, and then it would be ours."

"The entire house, as I remember, was reeking of damp."

"Only because it had been shut up for so long. The terrace was lovely—don't you remember?—sloping down to the river. You like sailing; you could keep a boat there and we could sail. There's a boathouse further down, past the orchard. And lots of fruit trees, but they may be dead now. And vines growing over the patio and . . ."

Her voice trailed into silence. What was the use of recalling the loveliness of the house? What was the use of discussing it? People could change their minds. He had said it was a firm decision, but when he went back to South America, perhaps they'd persuade him not to stay in Lisbon and—

"Before going back to South America," she heard him say, "I shall be going to Lisbon."

"To . . . to see about a house?"

"That wasn't the idea. Lord Tancred asked me whether—if he couldn't get anybody else to take Saint Christopher—I'd take it on my way back. I said I would. If I do, I'll speak about the Quinta do Rio to your aunt Pilar. Do you want me to cross my heart?"

She studied him.

"No. But are you . . . are you sure you'd like it?"

"An establishment of my own, with a pretty daughter growing up and acting hostess to my friends? A sailing boat, lunch on the terrace, drinks in the patio, sunset on the river, cats and dogs to trip over and birds singing in the trees. Are you sure I'd like it?"

She smiled. The smile widened, and became a laugh of pure happiness, and as he watched, she vanished and in her place sat her mother, and for the first time, he found that he could look without pain.

They drove home, reluctant to leave the peace of the riverside and return to the traffic of the town. As they passed a cinema, she touched his arm.

"Look. That's the film that was coming to Lisbon. The Pagets were going to see it if it came before we left for school."

He drew to the side of the road and stopped.

"Do you want to go now?"

"If you . . . yes, I'd like to very much."

He turned in his seat, studied the posters and gave a shudder.

"*The Last Scalp.* Starring Chuck Mackendrick. Oh God." He appealed to Tory. "Do I have to?"

"No. It's for children. Couldn't I go by myself?"

"Would you mind?"

"No. I'd like to."

He turned the car and brought it to a stop outside the cinema. He took out money and gave it to her.

"Sure you don't mind going alone?"

"Sure."

"You won't talk to any strangers who look like Mr. Darlan, will you?"

"No."

"And if anybody offers you poisoned chocolates or fancy drugs, you'll say you don't care for them, won't you?"

"Yes."

"Then off you go. I'll be here waiting when you come out."

She left him and went up the steps that led to the entrance. Then he saw her halt, turn, and come running back to the car.

"The front-door key." She took it out of her coat pocket and handed it to him. "If Philippa's out, you won't be able to get in without it."

He drove away. When he arrived at the house and saw Lord Tancred's car standing outside, he changed his mind about letting himself in, and rang the bell. Philippa came to the door.

"Where's Tory?" she asked, as he came in.

"Local cinema. I couldn't summon enough resolution to sit through *The Last Scalp.*" He entered the sitting room and nodded to Lord Tancred. "Any news?"

"None to speak of. I dropped in to tell Philippa what little there was. It's information of a kind, but it doesn't lead anywhere."

"Before you start talking, does anyone want tea, or a drink?" Philippa asked.

Nobody wanted either.

"No real progress," Lord Tancred went on. "They know a lot more about Madame Leblanc, but nothing that's interesting. The shop is a small clothing store. It's been going since she and her husband came from Normandy and started it fifteen years ago. He died, and she now runs it alone. She lives in the rooms above the shop. She's well known in the neighbourhood, not liked but apparently respected. She has no assistant, and can't leave the shop during working hours. At midday, she closes it and goes to lunch at a small restaurant in the same street—always the same restaurant, always the same table. She does her shopping very early in the morning, before opening the shop. On Sundays, she walks to Mass at the local church. As I said, nothing that leads anywhere—nothing that connects her with any kind of shady operations."

"Nothing but the basket," Edmund commented.

"Nothing but the basket. Her meeting with Tory, her anxiety to get hold of the basket, proves beyond doubt that she has some connection with Darlan—but if there is a connection, why are they not in touch? He was in Paris; he claimed his luggage. Now he seems to have disappeared. But if he doesn't get in touch with her, how can he learn what happened when Tory arrived at the Gare du Nord? The police think it unlikely that the statuette was the only object stolen; if there are other things, surely he must hand them over to her? The shop has been, is being watched. No Englishman with any resemblance to Darlan has been in or near it, or in the restaurant or at the church she goes to. So we're left with the unlikely situation that Darlan's in Paris but hasn't gone near

Madame Leblanc. It's so unlikely that it can't be true." He paused. "I don't mind admitting that my attitude to this affair has changed radically."

"Of course it has," Philippa said. "You started off by thinking that Tory was telling lies."

"I still think she kept something back—by intent, or because she didn't realize its significance. There's a piece missing. It doesn't look as though we're going to be able to make a whole picture out of the pieces we've got, and I shall always have a feeling that one of them remained in Tory's pocket." He rose and stood looking down at Philippa. "I've got to go. I only dropped in on the off chance of finding you in."

And of finding her alone, Edmund thought. Otherwise he would have kept the scraps of information about Madame Leblanc, and fed them to her at dinner.

"I'll call for you at eight," Lord Tancred told her.

Edmund saw him to the door, but instead of returning to the sitting room went to the kitchen, filled the kettle and put it on the stove.

"I'm taking you up on that offer of tea," he told Philippa as she came in. "Do you still use a mixture of Indian and China?"

"Yes." She pulled out a chair and sat down. "Tom's got his teeth into this, hasn't he?"

"He appears to have."

"What did you and Tory talk about?"

"Certainly not about her recent adventures. I think that if this inquiry weren't going on, or if you and I didn't ask her questions about what happened, we'd never hear her refer to the matter again. She acts as though it never took place."

"So would I have done, at her age. So would you. I can remember things happening when I was young which—I learned much later—rocked the household, but which made no impression on me. The only things that went deep, at Tory's age, were my agony at forgetting my lines in a school play and hearing the audience laughing—and seeing my puppy run over. And sitting down to an arithmetic exam and finding I couldn't do any of the questions. That all sounds trivial, but it's sometimes the things that adults think trivial that really upset children. The more I think about Tory's trip to England, the more convinced I am that Darlan said or did something to make her dislike him. He had to get out of the train to get something for his headache—that suggests a hangover. They'd had dinner together the night before; if he drank too much, or made an exhibition of himself, that would make any child loathe him. But it's something we'll never know, because if it had happened to me at that age I'm certain I would have kept it to myself." She got up to get cups and saucers, and took milk out of the refrigerator. "If you and she didn't talk about the past, did you discuss the future?"

"Yes. I told her that we were going to have a home of our own."

She looked at him in surprise. The look became speculative, and then searching.

"You mean that," she decided at last. "You're not just saying it—you mean it."

"Yes, I mean it. I suppose you realize that this business has been a shock?"

"If you mean that it's shaken you into a realization of what a poor parent you are, then yes, I suppose it was a shock. Any definite ideas about where you'd live?"

"I hadn't. Tory had. She pulled out of her hat a property I'd almost forgotten—a house on the other side of the Tagus, near Setubal."

"Would it do?"

"After I'd spent a fortune repairing it, yes, it would do very nicely."

"Then spend it. You're not poor—and Tory must have a lot of money coming to her one day from those old aunts."

He was pouring water into the teapot. He stopped, put back his head and gave one of his rare, unrestrained laughs.

"What's funny?" she asked. "There's that great house full of treasures and gold statuettes—that seems to me to be enough to keep her comfortable. Who's to inherit it, if she doesn't?"

"There'll be nothing to inherit."

She stared at him.

"All mortgaged?"

"Most of it. The house and the chapel will go to the Church. As for treasures, with the exception of the things in the chapel, which haven't been and won't be touched, there's been a steady sale of effects for years and years. And years. The family fortunes were founded on Brazilian gold. When the golden stream dried up, they fell back on the diamond mines. The family tradition's always been one of lavish spending, and it's still going on. I've never been able to estimate how much gets handed out to the various charitable organizations, but it must be a staggering sum. Pilar and Piedade act like Lisbon's richest old ladies. They don't give grand receptions anymore, but they give a series of what they call intimate parties, and the standard of entertainment is what it always has been: princely. Will you pour out, or shall I?"

"You. Go on talking. How can they give princely parties if the house has been denuded of its contents?"

"It's a shrinking process. Some of the rooms have been shut up for years. The lawyers hoped, when I settled down in the house, that I'd be able to put a check on the two sisters, but I never felt inside the family, and as an outsider I didn't feel I had a right to interfere. Not that any interference, from inside or out, would have stopped the rot." He stirred his tea thoughtfully. "It's an extraordinary atmosphere, that combination of past glory and present decay. Jesuina will die and have a splendid funeral. Pilar and Piedade will retire, in time, to some kind of convent—unless the house itself is turned into one, in which case they'll be saved the trouble of moving. But they'll never feel the pinch of poverty, because the remaining assets will last their lifetime. What Tory will get is what I can give her; it'll be adequate, thank God."

"Does she know all this?"

"Most of it."

"Who's this Mademoiselle Barrault she talks about?"

"She was given the courtesy title of governess—or French and music teacher—but rumour says that she came to Lisbon on the arm of Jesuina's husband. When he died, she stayed on and was eventually moved over to my part of the house to look after Tory's clothes and manners and what I suppose you could call cultural development. I thought once or twice of handing her back to Pilar and Piedade, but there's something appealing in the frank way she feathers her nest. Every dress she buys for Tory means one for herself, and the bills she hands me wouldn't bear close inspection, but I pay them because I feel that her worldliness, her cunning, her know-how were necessary antidotes to the excessive holiness of the aunts. Outwardly, Mademoiselle Barrault conforms; she doesn't miss any Masses or any confessions, but inwardly she's what she is, and I think Tory knows what she is."

"So will you take her along if and when you move to this house with Tory?"

"I think so. I'd miss the old cheat if I left her behind, and I think Tory would, too—so long as she was free of her ministrations."

"You're really serious about giving up the travelling part of the job?"

"Yes."

"You won't mind being stuck at a desk?"

He smiled.

"I don't know. You can put it down as a kind of penance."

"A nice thought. It's time you went to meet Tory at that cinema."

He glanced at the clock, and rose.

"Why don't you come, too?" he asked.

"No time. I have to have a bath and array myself in my best."

"For Tancred?"

"Why not? Think what he's doing for us."

"He's doing it for you."

"What's the difference, so long as he does it? With luck, we'll land that Darlan in prison and we won't even set eyes on a single policeman or a single detective. For that, I'd put on my most plunging neckline every time he takes me out."

"You might find yourself having the same kind of trouble with him as you had with your partner Douglas."

"Douglas only gave trouble because I said no."

"Is Tancred—"

"Is he what?"

"Nothing."

"If the question was 'Is he interested in renewing old acquaintance?' the answer's yes. Any comment?"

"Only that gratitude's not really a good base for matrimony."

"I'll make a note."

He went out, and she sat with her elbows on the table and her chin on her hands, staring at the two empty cups, while two words went round and round in her mind: Is he? Is he? Is he?

Is he interested in renewing old acquaintance, old affection, old love? How could one find out anything from a clam? Why was it that a man you didn't want wanted you, while a man you wanted, had always wanted, would always want with all your heart, gave no sign of wanting to renew anything and walked off leaving you to wash the cups? If gratitude wasn't a strong enough base, how about hope? How long could you go on hoping in the face of a total lack of interest or response? He was emerging from the past. He had spoken of his wife. He was planning a future with his daughter. If he was human, if he had a heart, if he even had eyes, wouldn't it strike him that a home needed a mistress, a child needed a mother, a man needed a woman?

Long, long ago, she had frankly pursued him. She had chased him and caught him—but she couldn't and wouldn't do it again. Too much had happened between those days and the present. He had loved another woman passionately, faithfully, long after she had been lost to him. How far he could forget, how far he could turn his thoughts to a future in which a dead wife had no part . . . who could guess? Nobody.

Once, twelve years before, she had succeeded in getting behind that calm, handsome facade. But he had been free. There had been no other woman, no other love, no other memory . . .

She rose, carried the cups to the sink and turned on the hot water. Let it flow away, flow away, flow away . . .

Chapter Nine

That day seemed to set a pattern for the three that followed. Each morning, Edmund appeared at the house for breakfast; after breakfast, he drove Philippa to work. He reappeared with the morning papers while Tory went out to play with Leo on the waste ground or to pay a brief visit to Mrs. Tesworth. She lunched with her father; Philippa lunched with Lord Tancred. There was no news from across the Channel; a watch was being kept on a small shop in Paris, but Mr. Darlan had not been seen in its vicinity.

On the fourth day, the pattern changed. Lord Tancred received a telephone summons from Paris, and flew there on a morning plane. His departure was a great relief to Edmund and Tory; to Philippa it was more; he was going too fast for her, and she needed time to think. He had never been a man to waste time, and he had not wasted any since their reunion. His mind, unlike hers, worked swiftly and efficiently; he knew what he wanted, he had told her what he wanted, and now she had to decide whether she would give him what he wanted. But with his departure came a perceptible closing of ranks; she freed herself from all engagements except those of spending her mornings at the shop, and outside working hours formed with Edmund and Tory a closely knit threesome.

Sunday brought the question of church: Catholic, Protestant or neither?

"You two might have a choice," Philippa said. "But I haven't. I'm on duty."

"In church?" Edmund asked in surprise. "Doing what?"

"Come and see. You might like the service, or you might not."

"Isn't it the usual morning service?"

"No. They call it a family service: father, mother and the children, and prams parked beside the pews. And guitars."

"Guitars?" Tory asked with interest.

"Yes. Interested?"

"Folk or classical?"

"Folk. Still interested?"

"Yes."

"Then let's go. It's off Colony Street, so the congregation's chessboard, that's to say black and white. If you want white only, you have to go in the other direction, where they haven't yet introduced whole-family services. Maybe you'd feel more at home there, Edmund, come to think of it; everybody well turned out, and a holy hush."

They went in the Colony Street direction. Philippa's duty, which she had undertaken to perform once a month, was to walk to the altar in procession with three housewives, carrying the Cross, the Chalice and the Host. The guitarists were two boys and two girls; they performed twice, before and after the reading of the lessons, and if the standard of playing and singing was not high, it was compensated for by the patent sincerity with which they claimed that God was comin', comin', comin' in His glory.

"Well?" Philippa asked on the way home.

"Interesting," Edmund said. "I'd like to know whether the parents were there because the children took them along."

"Of course. The drive's from the young," she told him. "I go to some of their meetings, so I know. They don't mind going along with the form of the old services, but they've cut out what they call the dirge and drone. It was this new Vicar who began it all. As soon as he arrived, the whole district sat up. Before he came, you could find a seat; now—as you saw—it's standing room only. Did you like it?"

"Some of it took my attention off what I like to think of as my devotions."

"Maybe you'll be awarded marks for trying. What I sometimes wonder is whether some of the angels have given up the harp and taken up the guitar. Nice change for them, but a bit of a surprise for God. I suppose we all look pretty odd from up there, walking in processions or wafting those ... Tory, what do you call those things they burn incense in?"

"Censers."

"Thank you. What I was going to say was that from a deity's point of view that can't look much odder than people going down on their knees and knocking their heads on the ground or on a prayer mat. Or wailing at a wall. Or sitting with their hands on their stomachs, gazing into space. One of the few compensations I can see about dying is to get up there and watch the streams flowing in from Rome and Canterbury or Mecca or Jerusalem or Nirvana, all flowing into one great river, which Tom Tancred would label the river of death, and file as an allegory. Tory, where shall we go and have lunch? You choose."

She chose the restaurant to which her father had taken her on his second day in England. It was a bitterly cold day, with a wind of such force that the car trembled at every intersection, but it proved a day of quiet contentment for all three. They cooked supper in the house, but as they were about to settle down to coffee or cocoa in the sitting room the telephone rang. Philippa answered it and came back to tell them that Fiona and her husband were together in their flat, and would welcome a talk with her.

"Only for an hour," Philippa promised. "They want to talk while Douglas is out of the way—he's spending the weekend in the country. It'll help if we can face him with some facts on which Fiona and I have agreed."

"I'll take you there," Edmund said.

"That's nice of you, but the bus stops just outside Fiona's door."

"I'll stop just outside Fiona's door, too. I can go back for you and bring you home."

"No. They'll do that, thanks all the same. Tory, say good night; you'll be in bed before I get back."

Her father had not returned when Tory went upstairs to get ready for bed. She heard the front doorbell, and went down again to answer it, wondering why her father had not used his key. But it was not her father who stood on the doorstep. It was Derek.

For some moments, she had difficulty in recognizing him. His face, under the hall light, looked yellow; his eyes were red-rimmed and swollen, and wiping away tears had left his cheeks grime-streaked. He spoke in an unsteady voice.

"Tory, you seen Leo anywhere?"

The colour left her cheeks. She opened the door wider, but he shook his head.

"Can't come in. No time. This is the last chance I've got to find him before I go. You seen him anywhere?"

"No. Not since we played this morning. Can't you . . . don't you know where . . . "

"He's lost." He paused to steady his voice. "He's been lost . . . "

"When did you last have him?"

"I came here with him, earlier on—I brought him in case you wanted to say good-bye, like, because there wouldn't be time to bring him tomorrow because the train goes at eleven, so I came here. I had him on his leash. I rang the bell, but nobody was in, so I took him for a last run round the waste ground, and we played for a bit, and then I walked to the road and stopped to wait for him, to put him on his leash again. But he didn't come. I called and whistled, but still he didn't come, and I couldn't see him on the waste ground, so I thought he'd gone on ahead somehow, and got onto the road. So I ran along as far as the shops, looking, and then I came back and went the other way, but he wasn't anywhere, and nobody'd seen him. He's lost."

The hopelessness, the despair in the last two words went to her heart.

"I'll go and look for him," she said without hesitation.

"You can't go now; it's too dark. If you find him tomorrow when I've gone, tell Mrs. T. She's upset."

"Look Derek, if you wait, I'll ask my father—"

She stopped. He had turned and run to the gate and into the road, swerving to avoid her father as he came towards the house. She stared after him in an agony of pity. He was going away in the morning, and he would have to go without Leo.

Her father came in and closed the door, and she looked up at him, tears in her eyes.

"What's wrong, Tory?"

"It was Derek. Leo's lost."

"That's unfortunate. Didn't you tell me they were going down to Eastbourne in the morning?"

"Yes. If he doesn't find Leo—"

"Any idea where he lost him?"

"On the waste ground. Derek's afraid he got onto the road, but he'd hear from somebody, wouldn't he, the police or somebody, if Leo'd been run over? Wouldn't he?"

"Not necessarily." Edmund looked down at her, frowning in helpless sympathy. "Would you like to drive round the streets and see if we can find him?"

"Oh, *could* we?"

"Put on every warm thing that you possess—it's freezing."

They drove slowly round the district, and round again, looking and calling and whistling. No Leo answered, no Leo appeared. At last, all hope gone, they returned to the house. He was surely, Tory decided, lying dead by the roadside. If he were alive, he would have found his way home. He was an intelligent little dog, and he knew his way round the neighbourhood; if he hadn't come home, he must be dead.

Before getting into bed, she went to the window to open it the inch or two she considered sufficient to keep the air in the bedroom fresh throughout the night. She felt no desire to sleep; her mind was on Leo, and on Leo's desolate owner.

She drew the curtains close, and was turning away when a sound reached her ears and made her stiffen.

A dog. A dog next door. A dog uttering yelps of distress. A dog? Leo.

She switched off the light and drew back a corner of the curtain. From the light streaming from the kitchen of the house next door, she saw a tall, angular figure emerge and guessed that it must be Mrs. Dexter. She was holding by the scruff of the neck the small, struggling form of Leo. She walked to the garden shed, opened the door, dropped the dog roughly inside and then closed and locked the door. Then Tory saw her re-enter the house.

She stood in the darkness, staring down at the darkened garden, her mind tracing the probable course of events. Leo had got into Mrs. Dexter's garden. He had got in by way of the hole that she had seen the two boys digging at the base of Mrs. Dexter's wall. It wouldn't have had to be a large hole for Leo, inquisitive and exploring, to wriggle through. He had been caught and kept in the house until night so that nobody could hear him barking or whining—and now, in the darkness, he had been brought out and locked away, and in the morning . . . She shuddered. Mrs. Dexter had threatened, and what she had threatened she would perform: In the morning, Leo would be taken to the vet and given an injection and he would die—painlessly, but he would die.

The cold, entering through the open inch of window, sent her shivering to bed. She lay turning over in her mind the possibilities of freeing the dog. The shed door was locked. It was not a flimsy shed and it was not a flimsy door. She thought of going downstairs and appealing to her father to go next door and tell Mrs. Dexter that he knew she had the dog and that she must give him up—but she was certain that Mrs. Dexter would not answer the doorbell. The police? If they accused her, she would show them the hole in the wall and tell them that she had warned the boys of the consequences of allowing animals to enter her garden. And by the time the police had been told, and had gone to see her, and had tried to make her give up the dog, it would be too late to get him to Derek before the train left for Eastbourne. The thought of Derek in the train, being borne away from a dog he believed lost to him forever, caused her tears to flow once more.

It was almost three o'clock before she slept. When she woke next morning, it was to find that Philippa and her father had left the house. She dressed and went downstairs. The table in the kitchen was laid with the things she would need for breakfast, but she did not feel like eating. Rage was filling her—helpless, hopeless rage. The manner in which the dog had been carried out of the house, the rough way in which it had been thrown on to the floor of the shed, made it seem certain that it had been kept without food or water. Would it do any good to telephone to the RSPCA? Would they come, and would they come at once? It was hopeless to expect that they would come before Mrs. Dexter had taken Leo to the vet.

She went upstairs and stood at her bedroom window, screened from view by the curtain. After what seemed to her an hour, she saw Mrs. Dexter come out of the house. She held her breath—but the shed was not Mrs. Dexter's objective. In her hand was a cardboard container filled with wastepaper and rags. She emptied it into a large incinerator standing in the corner of the garden close by the wooden fence that separated Philippa's house from her own. Then she took a box of matches from the pocket of her apron, and as she lit a match and applied it to the wastepaper, Tory realized that this was a day on which the wind would carry charred fragments into Philippa's garden. Not even Mrs. Dexter's determination to take the dog to be destroyed could prevent her from lighting a fire in the incinerator and preparing her neighbourly act.

Tory saw her re-enter the house. She emerged in a short while, and, to Tory's immense relief, she was carrying a shopping basket. She was going out, going to fetch the bread and the milk—not from the local shops, because Philippa had said that she had quarrelled with them—but from shops to which she had to go by bus. How long would she be away? Five minutes to the bus, ten minutes on the bus, say twenty minutes to do her shopping, then ten minutes back again, and five to walk down the road to her house. About three quarters of an hour; with luck, an hour. Only an hour. What could be done in an hour to save Leo?

If she got a ladder and climbed over the fence, would she manage to push open, break open the door of the shed? She decided to make the attempt. She ran downstairs, drew out the stepladder from the cupboard below the stairs, put on her coat and went into the garden. Already, burnt pieces of paper were floating over the hedge and settling on Philippa's flower beds. At the foot of the wall lay the previous day's total of rubbish thrown over by passing schoolboys: a bicycle tire, two car tires, an old blanket, two old felt hats.

She placed the stepladder in position, climbed up and looked down into Mrs. Dexter's garden. Immediately below her she could see the flames, now low, now leaping, in the incinerator. She was about to move the stepladder farther along, when she paused. Her heart began to beat faster. She closed her eyes; she had to think . . . think . . . think . . .

She opened her eyes. Would it work? If it worked, would they come? They had to come, didn't they, if they were summoned? They had to. It all depended on whether she could . . .

She ran into the house. From the cupboard she took out every newspaper she could find. Climbing up the stepladder once more, she leaned over and dropped them, one by one, into the incinerator. Then she got down and fetched several items from the junk pile. She carried the bicycle tire up the ladder and then dropped it on to the smouldering newspapers. Would it burn? The newspapers had caught; here came the flames. Next, the blanket. Then the felt hats. And now for the car tire. It was very heavy. Would it burn? Would it send up thick, black smoke, as she had seen old car tires do in Lisbon when the chauffeur had burned them in a corner of the courtyard?

She lowered the tire as far as she could, and then dropped it. It fell squarely on to the now-burning hats.

She went back to the house and put away the stepladder. Would there be smoke? Please, Lord . . . was it Our Lord's week or Our Lady's week? Hail Mary, full of grace . . . Oh God, please make a lot of smoke.

Standing by the back door, she watched—and then her heart

leapt with the column of black smoke that rose from the garden next door. Higher, higher . . . Hail Mary . . . blacker and blacker. Now she could go out. Take a shopping basket and go to the shops and wait . . . and go on praying.

When she reached the corner, she glanced back, and her heart lifted in triumph. From the back of Mrs. Dexter's house was rising a high, steady column of black smoke. The column thickened and spread. She walked on and entered the grocer's shop. Someone would telephone. Not herself; the less she appeared to know about this, the better. Would it burn on, blacker and blacker? The minutes were passing—why didn't somebody make that call? Surely people realized that it was their duty to pick up a phone, or to find the nearest fire alarm, when they saw . . .

And then, at last, she heard it. She joined the grocer and his customers in the doorway, and with eyes bright with relief watched the shining equipage thunder by, its siren sounding a double warning signal, the golden helmets glinting under the wintry sun. It went round the corner into Elcombe Grove, and the grocer glanced at Tory.

"Looks as though it's near Miss Brackley's house," he told her. "You'd better go and take a look."

She stopped to pay for her purchases, and then she left the shop and went in the wake of the sightseers who were making their way up Elcombe Grove. Outside Mrs. Dexter's house was the fire engine; the firemen had already carried a hose through the front garden to the back.

Tory, reaching the gate, did not hesitate. She pushed her way through the knot of spectators, slipped round a policeman and was brought up short by a fireman.

"Can't come any nearer," he informed her. "You'd better get back."

"Please . . . there's a dog in that shed. Will you get him out?"

He glanced at the shed; she was already at the door, calling Leo. His answering howls rose over the confusion reigning in the garden.

"Key?" the fireman enquired.

She shook her head.

"I haven't got it. It—"

There was no need to explain. The fireman had raised a booted leg and with a single thrust had sent it crashing through the wooden door. A second kick, and there was room for Tory to crawl through. She lifted out the whimpering little dog and held him firmly under her arm. Nobody showed any interest in her as she went out through the gate.

She let herself into Philippa's house and went at once to the kitchen. She poured milk into a deep ashtray and set it before Leo. He drank, finished it and begged for more. She gave him some more and then opened the can of dog meat she had brought from the grocer's. He ate half the contents, and would have eaten the other half if Tory had not felt that he had had enough. She put the half-empty can into the trash can. From a shelf in the hall she lifted down a small picnic hamper; into this, having run out of newspapers, she placed some sheets of Philippa's writing paper. Then she patted Leo, explained that the confinement would not last long, lifted him gently in and closed the lid. Holding the hamper firmly, she walked out of the house, crossed the road, skirted the boys' school, regretting that none of the boys had been at liberty to see the fire engine, and stopped at the corner to signal a passing taxi. Getting in, she directed the man to drive to Victoria Station.

He could not go fast; the streets were full of traffic. How long would it take to get there? It was past ten, and the train would go at eleven. Ten thirty. A quarter to eleven . . .

They had arrived. She paid the driver, clutched the hamper and ran as fast as she could into the station. She must keep her head; it was no use rushing about asking people who didn't know. The thing to do was to look at that board that said where the trains were.

Eastbourne: number three. She reached the barrier, and stopped. The train looked very long. It was due to leave in three minutes; how could she hope to find Derek? There was no time to walk down the platform looking into every carriage.

Then she saw him. He was standing beside one of the carriage doors, his hands thrust into his pockets, staring down in despair at the platform. From a loudspeaker came a voice stating that the train was about to leave, and he moved to board it.

Tory put the hamper on the ground, opened it and lifted out Leo. She held him with his head in Derek's direction. Would he see him? It was quite far. Could he . . .

Suddenly she felt the tensing of the small body. There was a moment of stillness and then a wild struggle for freedom which told her that he had seen his master. She released him, and he raced along beside the train, yelping ecstatically, streaking past the legs of passersby, bounding over luggage.

She waited only to see the leap with which he hurled himself into Derek's arms. Then she picked up the hamper and walked to the exit. She had no wish to be seen. It had worked, but she wasn't going to tell anybody anything about it. She was happy, and so was Derek and so was Leo, and it wasn't anybody's business but her own. The thing to do was to be glad that it had worked—and forget it. And take a bus home. No, not a bus; a taxi. She must be home before her father, or not long after.

She had leisure, on the way back, to review the morning's events, and weighed for a time the idea of telling Philippa what she had done. She was certain that Philippa would have approved the methods used in restoring Leo to his owner; like herself, she would have understood that the thing had to be done in a hurry, and that official channels would have taken too long and been too late. But telling Philippa was one thing; expecting her to keep it a secret was another. That was the great disadvantage of confiding in grown-ups; they might sympathize, they might condone, they might even applaud, but there was always a reason why they had to pass on the information. Philippa might or might not pass it on to Tory's father, but even if she didn't, experience had taught that the best way of avoiding complications was to keep her own counsel. There was nothing to connect her with the morning's fire; the fireman might say—if Mrs. Dexter asked him—that he had smashed the shed door at the request of a little girl, but as she was totally unknown to Mrs. Dexter, his description of the little girl would lead nowhere. Tell her father? No. Not her father. She didn't really know him yet, and he didn't really know her. Things between them were getting better and, she hoped and believed, would go on getting better; it would be a pity to risk straining at the outset a relationship that promised so much.

She had asked the driver to stop at the end of Elcombe Grove; now, changing her mind, she directed him to Colony Street; there would just be time to go and tell Mrs. Tesworth that Leo had been found; that would put her mind at rest. She paid the taxi and hurried down the now-familiar steps, but when she knocked on Mrs. Tesworth's door there was no response. Knocking again, she heard the curtain being drawn back; the door opened and she saw not Mrs. Tesworth but Mr. Barlow.

"Good morning." She spoke in haste. "I can't stay; I only came to tell Mrs. Tesworth that Leo was found." He seemed to have difficulty in taking in what she said, and she spoke more urgently. "Leo. He was found. He went on the train with Derek."

From behind Mr. Barlow a wheezy voice spoke.

"You sure, ducks?"

Tory raised her voice.

"Yes, Mrs. Tesworth, I'm quite sure. They both went off together."

No reply came from within the room. Mr. Barlow put a gentle hand on her shoulder.

"She's not too well," he explained. "She's got to keep to her bed for a day or two. Thank you for coming to tell her."

The door was already closing. Tory went away as swiftly as she had come; she had given the message and Mrs. Tesworth could now feel happy; it was a pity she hadn't been feeling well, but it had saved being asked a lot of awkward questions about how she knew that Leo had gone on the train with Derek.

Turning the corner into Elcombe Grove, she saw no sign that any fire engine had ever been there. Nor, to her relief, was her father's car at the gate of number fourteen. Only after she had put the picnic hamper back on the shelf and washed the ashtray and put the writing paper in the trash can did she hear his car stop at the gate. She opened the door and he came in and bent to kiss her.

"Good morning. Philippa and I went up to look at you this morning. You were sleeping peacefully. Been out?"

"Yes."

"They told me at the paper shop that there's been a lot of excitement next door—a fire. You must have had a good view from your bedroom window."

"I was out when the fire engine came. I saw it go by when I was in the grocer's shop."

"Mrs. Dexter burning car tires, I heard, but she's blaming it on the schoolboys. I don't see how they could have got over that high wall—and they certainly wouldn't risk going in the front way. The general feeling seemed to be that she did it to try to get the boys into trouble."

"It's awfully cold today; would you like me to make you some hot coffee?"

"Yes, please. We're meeting Philippa for lunch. I've booked a table at the Portuguese restaurant in Coombe Street—it's new and it's said to be good." He followed her into the kitchen and sat watching her as she made coffee for him and cocoa for herself. "Only three days more," he said regretfully. "Are you looking forward to getting to a new school, or do you hate the idea?"

"Do they let you take pets? Philippa didn't know for certain."

"We could ask them."

She shook her head.

"No. They'd only allow things like guinea pigs and white mice and things, and I don't like those. If we ever got a house of our own, we could have cats and dogs, couldn't we?"

"We could, and it isn't a case of 'ever having' a house of our own. I made a deal with you, and I'm sticking to it. By the way, did your young friend find his dog?"

"Yes, he did."

"Good. I'm glad. I lost a dog once, and I know exactly how he must have felt—how your young friend must have felt, I mean."

"Did you find him again?"

"The police found him. He'd been chasing a lady dog and had lost his way. Speaking of that house of our own, I wrote to your aunt Pilar last night. About selling the Quinta do Rio."

"Do you think she will?"

"I think she'll be only too glad to." He took his cup from her. "Do you ever think about family finances? Or don't they interest you?"

"You mean ours, or Aunt Pilar and Aunt Piedade's?"

"Theirs. I don't suppose they've ever mentioned them to you, but I've sometimes wondered whether Mademoiselle Barrault discussed them. Did she?"

Tory stirred her cocoa and wondered how much of Mademoiselle Barrault's information it would be prudent to reveal. Not much, she decided. Mademoiselle Barrault blamed Jesuina for most of the misfortunes that had befallen the Casa Fenix during the past forty years, but her revelations were made in the form of innuendo or insinuation and covered more than finance. It was no use getting Mademoiselle Barrault into trouble; she had her drawbacks but she also had her uses.

"What she told me," she said at last, "was that there were debts. Lots of debts."

"Anything else?"

"She says that they can never be paid off, so one day the house will be sold and the people who are owed the money will share it out, but there won't be any left for me."

"Did that worry you?"

"No."

"Would you have liked the house to be yours one day?"

"No."

"Why not?"

"It isn't . . . it isn't like a house that other people live in. It's not a homey house. I only like the chapel. I wish the chapel could be separate, but it can't, can it? I mean, that'll go, too."

"Yes. From the very beginning, when it was first built, it was promised to the Church. Nothing in it was ever to be removed or sold. I think that when Jesuina dies the Church will take over the whole place, house and chapel, and your aunts will go on living in it, as women used to do in the old days, taking no vows but contributing to the general funds, and ending their lives in dignity and comfort."

"Can their relations go to visit them?"

"Their relations and their friends, yes."

"Would they be able to entertain people?"

"They did in those old days I mentioned, but I'm not sure how much would be allowed today."

They fell silent—a companionable silence, Tory noted with interest and pleasure. She felt warm and contented and at ease. Derek had Leo, she had her father, and today there was also Philippa.

Contentment was the keynote of the day. The restaurant was genuinely Portuguese and the weather, when they emerged, so unexpectedly warm and sunny that they drove to the park and walked beside the water until the sun's warmth faded and it was time to go home. Nobody wanted to go out again, and all three did their share in the preparation of supper. At last, reluctantly, Tory realized that it was time for bed.

"Can I come down again and say good night?" she asked her father.

"Yes."

"Can I have a shower?"

"Immediately after a meal?"

"It won't hurt. I'll wash my hair, too."

When she had gone, Philippa made coffee and went with Edmund into the sitting room.

"Odd that Tancred's not back," he commented. "I thought he was only going to be away for a day."

"Nobody stated any definite period. I suppose he's waiting to see if they find out anything. I'm beginning to be sorry I got him into this."

"I don't think he's sorry. Are you—"

"Am I what?"

"Are you thinking of marrying him?"

"I'm only thinking. As my oldest friend, why don't you give me some advice?"

"You're a free agent."

"Thanks to you. Do you ever feel twinges of remorse, like Tom?"

"Yes. I always did, and not only twinges. I loved you. What happened in Macau was—"

"Inevitable. I know. I'm glad you were happy. Tom wasn't, and I wasn't, but those years you had seem to me to make up for a lot. And you've got Tory. You won't go back on that promise to get her a home, will you?"

"No. As your oldest friend, could I ask whether Tancred has said anything definite?"

"About wanting to marry me? Of course he has. Is he the kind of man who'd hold back if there was something he wanted?"

"What are you going to decide?"

"Well, I'd like to get married; that much I'm sure about. I don't understand career women. If it's a choice between earning my own living and sitting in a nice home waiting for my husband to put a fat pay check in my outheld hand, give me the man and the money. So I'll get married."

"To Tancred?"

"I'll shuffle the pack, pick a card and see what comes out." She rose lazily, put out a hand and pulled him to his feet. "All this discussion about marriage has warmed my blood. Kiss me."

He kissed her, but his arms did not close round her. After a moment, she released him.

"That felt just like an oldest friend," she told him. "Go and get me some more coffee, if there's any left."

He took his cup and hers and went without a word, and she leaned against the open door and closed her eyes and let hope drain slowly out of her. Twelve years. And years before those twelve years, when she had been growing up. She had loved him for longer than she could remember. Then he had gone away, and he had never come back. He was here now in body, but she couldn't reach his mind, his thoughts, his heart. She couldn't blame him for being faithful to a memory; memory, in his case, had at least something to feed on. But in her own case, what was there? Nothing. He was here, and she had shown him as openly as she could that her feelings about him were what they had always been. She couldn't do any more. She had done something, perhaps more than they both knew, to prepare him for a happy life with Tory. He would make a home for his daughter, but in it, apart from visits, there would be no place for herself.

She heard him returning and went back to her chair. He placed her cup on a small table and stood looking down at her.

"Philippa—"

He broke off. Footsteps had sounded outside on the path. The next moment, the doorbell rang.

"I'll go," Edmund said.

She rose, a feeling of uneasiness rising in her mind. She heard the front door open and close. Then Lord Tancred was in the room, and as soon as she saw his expression, she spoke with conviction.

"Something's happened. Something bad."

"Yes." He glanced at her cup. "Is there still some hot coffee?"

"I'll get it," Edmund said.

Nothing was said while he was out of the room. Lord Tancred was lost in thought. Philippa was doing her best to guess what bad news he had brought.

Edmund returned with a large cup of coffee in one hand and a bottle of brandy in the other.

"Thanks. I need that." Lord Tancred added a liberal helping of brandy to the coffee, and drank it. He put down the cup with a sigh of relief.

"I was cold right through," he said. "I've had two bad days."

"What happened?" Philippa asked.

"Madame Leblanc is dead. Murdered."

There was silence. Lord Tancred sat down, pushed back his hair with both hands and answered the unspoken questions.

"I told you," he said, "that the shop, and the rooms above it in which she lived, were being watched. Some time, sooner or later, it was certain that Darlan would make contact. He did. But in spite of the watch that was being kept, he was not seen going in—or leaving. It's now not a case of trying to lay hands on a thief. All the signs are that he killed her."

"What signs?" Edmund asked.

"First, let me go back a bit. Darlan had got in touch with her from Lisbon; he arranged to meet her at the Gare du Nord, and he undoubtedly told her that he was bringing the statuette with him. The reason she wasn't going on to London with him is now clear: She operated from Paris. That has now been established."

"Murdered! But . . . but why?" Philippa asked.

"They were associates. The police were watching her place, but there was nothing to give them a pretext to enter or to search. They were looking for an Englishman answering Darlan's description. He didn't appear. Yesterday morning, Madame Leblanc failed to open the shop. As the police knew she had gone up to her rooms as usual the night before, they investigated. After they had investigated, they telephoned and asked me to go over there. When I arrived, they told me the details. She was found, still in her day clothes, lying on the floor of her sitting room. She'd been hit on the head, brutally, by a heavy candlestick. The murderer didn't have to go far to get hold of one—there were twenty-six of them hidden in the apartment. Tall, heavy, beautiful, silver or gold candlesticks. And on examining the one which had been used to kill her, they found traces of—"

"The golf bag," Edmund said.

"Yes. What made you think of it?"

"It's been at the back of my mind ever since this thing started. There was something that didn't fit about the golf angle. He came out every year to play golf—but he didn't play much. It seemed more and more odd, when I thought about it, that he laid so much stress on the game: the golfer's hotel, the golf club at Estoril, the seeking out of other golfers. I thought of the golf bag, but only while you were speaking just now did I realize that it must have been used to hide the things he stole."

"It was a simple plan," Lord Tancred said. "So simple that it worked. It worked smoothly for years. Trace Darlan's movements, as the police are doing now, and you'll find he was in all the places from which reports came in of candlesticks being stolen from churches. Easy to carry in the golf bag. Easy to carry, and easy to dispose of."

"But not easy to get," Philippa objected. "How could he walk into churches and come out with two-feet-long candlesticks without being seen?"

"I don't know—but that's what he did," Lord Tancred said. "I think that when he was shown round the Casa Fenix and entered the chapel the first thing his eyes would have gone to were the candlesticks."

"No. If he entered from the house, which he did," Edmund said, "he would have found himself looking straight across at the niches in which the golden statuettes stand. I don't think he would have thought about candlesticks after seeing those. But I think he'd heard about the Saint Christopher, and had decided to steal it when he telephoned to offer himself as escort to Tory. The thing is, when could he have done it?"

"I can tell you how," Lord Tancred said. "He managed to get past the guard at the gate. Guards have to leave their posts sometimes. He may have forgotten to lock the gate. He may have been bribed to forget."

"Not possible," Edmund said. "If ever Guilhermo had to leave the gate, one of his sons took over. When he had his meals, his wife sat on guard. They're all—father, mother, son—absolutely above suspicion."

"Then Darlan will have to explain how he got in—when they catch him. But Philippa asked why he had to go as far as murder. Take the sequence of events: He lost the train at Bayonne, he telephoned from there to Madame Leblanc and told her she had to meet Tory at Austerlitz and get that basket from her. When he arrives and gets in touch with her, she shows him the empty basket and tells him a story of its having been left in the cloakroom, empty. It wouldn't have sounded very convincing. The candlestick that killed her was lying beside her, and he didn't stop to remove fingerprints. If they find him, they'll have enough to convict. If they find him. But he seems to be—"

He stopped. Tory was on her way downstairs.

"I think it's unnecessary to tell her everything," Edmund said in a low voice.

Lord Tancred nodded. Tory came in, greeted him quietly, and addressed her father.

"I've only come to say good night."

"Don't go for a minute," Edmund said. "Lord Tancred's got some news."

She settled herself on a stool at his feet, in pajamas with Philippa's jacket over them, her hair still damp but smoothly brushed. It was the first time she had elected to lean against his knees, rather than against Philippa's, and a strange, warm feeling of pleasure crept over him.

Lord Tancred spoke from across the room.

"The French police," he told Tory, "now know that Mr. Darlan is a thief."

She looked up at him.

"They know he took the Saint Christopher?"

"He took more than that. They're looking for him because he's been going round for years stealing candlesticks and hiding them in his golf bag."

"Candlesticks?"

"Yes. Hidden in his golf bag. Which explains why he rushed out of the train at Bayonne. He didn't want anybody to look too closely at it."

She said nothing. She appeared lost in thought, slowly untying the lace of one of Edmund's shoes.

"Candlesticks?" She half turned and looked up at her father. "Just candlesticks?"

"Yes," he said. "Easy to hide in his golf bag. He seems to have had a liking for things ecclesiastical. It explains his annual visits to Portugal and to other countries where there were churches and chapels, richly endowed, full of candlesticks."

"But I still don't see how he could take them away," Philippa said. "He'd hardly take his golf bag into a church with him, would he? So I don't—"

She caught sight of Tory's expression, and stopped. Tory was looking at her, but she was seeing something beyond her. She spoke slowly, almost dreamily.

"It wasn't a prayer book," she said. "And it wasn't a Bible. It was a missal."

"A—?" For a moment, Lord Tancred was at a loss. "Oh, a missal, yes. The Catholic Masses for the year. But I don't quite see what that has to do with what Philippa was saying."

Tory appeared not to have heard the interruption.

"He wasn't a Catholic," she went on. "But he had a missal. I saw it."

"Where?" Edmund asked, and kept his voice deliberately calm. "Where did you see it?"

"I saw it in his suitcase, when he had to open it at Hendaye. I thought it was a prayer book, or a Bible, but it wasn't. It was a missal."

"Why would he have packed a missal in his luggage?" Edmund asked. "You could have been mistaken."

She turned fully round to face him, but when she spoke, there was no emphasis or excitement in her voice. She was following a thread, throwing her mind back, reviewing what she had seen in the suitcase but failed to see clearly.

"I *was* mistaken," she said. "I thought it was a Bible, but it wasn't. And I thought it was a dressing gown, but it wasn't. A dressing gown wouldn't have a black lining. And I thought he had a hat packed, a hat with a wide brim, but it wasn't. Don't you see? He couldn't have got past Angelina and the maids, because they would have known he'd come in the wrong way. So he must have got in the other way, from the road, through the courtyard, and how could he have got past Guilhermo? That's why it wasn't a Bible, it was a missal, and it wasn't a dressing gown, and it wasn't an ordinary hat. And those black shoes . . . there were black shoes, too. Daddy, don't you see?"

Edmund took her hand.

"Yes, Tory. Yes, I see."

"And that's why Jesuina was crying, because she'd seen him and she thought he was a priest, and so she couldn't tell anybody, don't you see? He was a priest, and so Guilhermo let him in. It was only a dressing gown on one side, and on the other side, it was a black robe."

She stopped. Nobody spoke. The puzzled look had left her forehead. She retied the lace of her father's shoe, got to her feet, kissed him and Philippa and shook hands with Lord Tancred. Then she went into the hall and up the stairs, and in silence they listened to her footsteps and the closing of her bedroom door. Then Lord Tancred spoke slowly.

"So now," he said, "they know what to look for."

Chapter Ten

Three days, two days. One day. They passed with the rhythm, the relentlessness of a countdown. The last day came, and Tory told herself that she was not sorry.

Accustomed throughout her life to drawing up her own balance of accounts, inured to finding roadblocks where she had hoped to proceed freely, she had no difficulty now in summing up her conclusions. Things could have been worse—much, much worse. There could, for instance, have been no Philippa. To have hoped for more than the meetings at the beginning and end of the school terms would have been a denial of something she had grown to accept from babyhood: the fact of her father's devotion to her mother, or to her mother's memory.

The thought was terrible, but if one knew Philippa one could cling to the steadying fact that what she promised, she performed. And she had promised, not once but many times, to stay within reach. That was to say, if Tory needed her, she would be there; if she wasn't actually there, she would get there as soon as she could.

Dreams. Tory, walking for the last time across the waste ground, dressed in her school clothes, wearing her school beret with its badge, thought about dreams. She had left Philippa in the house. Philippa had not gone to work that morning because she was going to drive to the school with Tory and her father. She had called to Tory from her room to say that she was not feeling well and would stay in bed for a little while, and didn't want any breakfast.

Dreams. Pausing absently to look at Mrs. Dexter's wall, the hole in it now firmly closed and cemented, she decided that it didn't do to dream too much about things that couldn't come true, like, for instance, having Philippa forever at the Quinta do Rio. If you thought about that too much, you didn't get anywhere and you got too upset. The things to remember were that she, Tory, was going to live with her father in a wonderful house, once they'd bought it and repaired it, and they were going to have dogs and cats and any other animals she wanted, short of zoo ones. She'd see Philippa at the beginning and the end of every school term—that was six times a year; it could be more if she came out to Portugal to visit them, but if she got married to Lord Tancred she'd better leave him behind, because nobody wanted him. It was terrible if you looked at things the way they could have been, but if you concentrated on what there was, it didn't look too bad.

She turned in the direction of Colony Street; she had to say good-bye to Mrs. Tesworth. She had not been to the house since the morning of Derek's departure. If Mr. Barlow wasn't there, she would leave a farewell message for him. But he was there, and the leavetaking did not take long. Tory promised that she would visit them on her return from school; then she left them.

The house in Elcombe Grove seemed empty. As she let herself in, she saw in the hall her suitcases—two, since the one she had brought with her had proved too small to fit her new books and the dressing gown that Philippa had bought her, and the skates her father had given her because the school had a pond that froze. If it froze, then it must be frozen now, because it couldn't be much colder than this, even in the Arctic. This was the last time she would use her latchkey—until the end of term. In an hour, her father was coming to drive her to the school, and then he was going to fly to Lisbon with Saint Christopher, and somebody was going with him to get the statuette through the Customs. And then he was going to arrange everything—the house, the repairs, the furniture, and it would be wonderful, only Philippa wouldn't be there.

Philippa didn't seem to be here, either. She wasn't in the sitting room and she wasn't in the kitchen, but she couldn't have gone out, because the morning paper was still where the paper boy had put it—thrust halfway through the letter box. She took it out and laid it beside Philippa's plate. When she came down . . .

She heard movements upstairs. She went into the hall and was halfway up the stairs when she heard something else: Philippa was crying.

She stood outside the door, and after a while she found herself trembling at the sound of the wild grief that could be heard, could almost be felt through the panels. She raised a hand to knock, but could not find the courage; then, with an effort, she managed it. The sobs ceased.

"Philippa . . . "

"Just a minute. I'm—I'm coming, Tory."

"Can I come in?"

"If you want to. I don't look very beautiful."

Tory, going in, could not think this anything but an understatement. Philippa's eyes were red and swollen, her hair disarranged, her cheeks tear-streaked. She was at the dressing table, attempting to repair her makeup; she gave Tory a wavering smile in the mirror.

"I thought you were out," she said.

"I was. I came back. Philippa, what's the matter?"

"The matter"—Philippa's tone was steady, and grew resolute—"is that I'm a born idiot. I'm crazy. And I'm ungrateful, because I don't realize when I'm well off. Tory"—she put down the jar of face cream she was holding and turned to face Tory—"sit on the bed, will you? I've something to say."

Tory remained standing.

"I know what it is, I think," she said. "Is it about marrying Lord Tancred?"

"Yes. Has it been so obvious?"

"I knew about him. I mean, I knew, I could see he wanted to. I wasn't sure whether you would or not."

"And I wasn't sure either, Tory. But now I am. And I don't know how much I ought to talk to you about it, because, although you've never seemed like a child, looking at you now I can see that you're only a ten-year-old and your concern is with going to school and being happy and learning a lot and having a lovely home in Portugal to go to. You're going to be very happy, and I'm happy for you."

"Then why were you crying?"

"I told you—because I'm off my head. Would any other woman cry because a man like Lord Tancred loves her and wants to marry her?" She rose, came to sit on the bed and drew Tory down beside her. "Will you listen carefully? I had a difficult decision to make, but I've made it. I'm going to marry Lord Tancred. I told him so last night. He's coming here soon to take me out, because I couldn't face driving to school with you and . . . and your father. I couldn't. I'm sorry. I said good-bye to your father and I'm going to say good-bye to you as soon as I've got myself looking decent enough to go out. I'm going to the shop to break the news to Douglas and Fiona. And then I'm going up to Scotland with Lord Tancred. I'm marrying him, Tory darling, because I don't want to waste my life . . . any more years of my life . . . looking back on something that's dead and will never come to life again. I wish I could explain this better, but perhaps you can understand what I'm trying to say. Every person is different. Your father loved your mother very much, and still does, and that means that he'll never move on, never move away from that memory. He's happy remembering; he doesn't need anything or anybody to fill her place, because her place isn't empty. But I can't be like him, Tory. I could, but I won't. I won't, I won't. I don't want to live with my eyes on the past. I'm going to marry Lord Tancred because that'll mean a new life, a full life, going forward, leaving behind a set of memories which have acted like a brake on me for more years than I can count. I don't want to live on memories, like your father. I don't want to feed on a dead passion, if you can understand that. I'm saying this to you because the one thing I want to keep with me when I leave this house is you. I want to have you for as many holidays as you'll be allowed to spend with me. You're the only child I'll ever have . . . and in a way, you might have been mine. So Tory—"

She stopped. The tears were pouring down her cheeks. Tory, after one glance, fixed her eyes desperately on the flowers on the dressing table. Words welled up in her throat and choked her. She would have given the world to speak, to move, to indicate what she was feeling. She wanted to say that she, too, wanted to go forward with Philippa, wanted to keep the link between them unbroken —but she was powerless to express what she was feeling, for beneath the hope was despair. Philippa was going. Her future would be with Lord Tancred, with whom Tory would never enjoy friendship, let alone affection. He would take Philippa away, and that would be the end, and she would be left with her father —and her mother's memory.

Philippa was watching her. After a while, she leaned forward and kissed her lightly.

"You're like your father, Tory. You can't pull words out from the deep places. Fight it. Fight it, Tory. Practice reaching out to people you love. If you don't reach out, if you don't express what you're feeling, how can they ever know?" She got up and went to the dressing table. She picked up the framed photograph of Tory's father, took it out of its frame, tore it slowly across and dropped the two halves into the wastepaper basket. "There. A safety measure." She picked up the little koala bear and dropped it beside the torn photograph. "Two safety measures. That's my past, Tory. I would have liked to go back, but as I can't, I'm going forward. And now will you do something for me? Will you go down and make me the strongest cup of coffee you can?"

Dazed, her legs feeling weak, Tory went down to the kitchen. She had the coffee ready when Philippa came downstairs. Standing by the table, Philippa picked up the cup and began to sip the scalding hot liquid. Then she put the cup down and spoke.

"There's some news I have to tell you, Tory. Lord Tancred got it yesterday evening. Your father knows what it is, but they felt it would be better if I told you this morning, in case there's anything in the papers and you hear about it at school. It's about Mr. Darlan."

"Yes?"

"He's dead. He died in a street accident. The police had found out who he was, and they wanted to question him. There was a chase, and he ran across a road and he was killed."

The kitchen faded from Tory's mind, and another scene took its place: a French railway station across which a man, an Englishman named Darlan, was running. That was how he must have run across the street—in panic, stumbling in his haste, recovering and running on. At Bayonne, he had been the pursuer, but on that street in Paris he was the pursued. The police had not caught him. He was dead. He could never answer their questions, never again steal candlesticks or golden statuettes. She tried to imagine him dead, but his image was fading, and she knew that if ever, in the future, she remembered him, it would be as she had seen him across the table of a dining car. But even that picture was growing dim.

Philippa was speaking.

"Come to the door with me, Tory, and then close it very quickly. That's the way to say good-bye. I won't come back until after you've gone. When Lord Tancred comes, tell him where I am, will you? He can pick me up there. And remember that the school term's going to be over soon, and I'll come and fetch you and it'll be spring and ... " She bent and kissed Tory's cheek. "Good-bye. Good-bye for now."

She was gone. Tory stood in the hall staring at the closed door, and then turned and went slowly up the stairs. From Philippa's wastepaper basket she took the koala bear and the two halves of her father's photograph. She went downstairs, opened one of her suitcases, took out gummed paper and scissors and went into the sitting room. Seated at the table, she put the torn pieces of the photograph and the bear in front of her, and began to paste the photograph together.

She was still at work when her father arrived. He did not use his key. He rang the bell, and she let him in. He followed her into the sitting room, stopping just inside the doorway, his eyes on her, a frown creasing his forehead.

"Tory, did Philippa tell you—"

That she's going to marry Lord Tancred?

"—the news about Mr. Darlan?"

"Yes."

"There wasn't much chance of its being reported in the English papers, but I thought you ought to know. I'm sorry he'd dead, but I'm glad that you can go back to school knowing that the whole thing's over and done with. I came early because the traffic's pretty heavy. We ought to allow ourselves plenty of time. Are you ready?"

"Yes. Practically."

She walked to the table and began to tidy up the work she had been doing.

"What's that?" her father asked from behind her.

She did not turn.

"I was trying to stick this together."

He had come forward and was staring down at the torn pieces of photograph.

"Did you do that?"

"No. Philippa did, just now."

"Is she . . . is she here?"

"No. She didn't feel well this morning. Then she felt better and she said good-bye to me and went to the shop to tell them she was going to marry Lord Tancred and go up to Scotland with him."

"Where did you find this . . . these . . . "

"She talked to me upstairs. She was crying. Then she tore this up and put it into the wastepaper basket with the koala bear, so I took them out and I was just sticking the pieces together."

"When did she tell you she was going to . . . "

"She told me when I went into her room, when she was crying."

There was silence. Her eyes were on the work she had been

doing, but she had forgotten it. She was waiting. When nothing came, she took another despairing step.

"She was crying because she didn't want to be like you."

"Like me?"

"She said that if she let herself, she could live on memories, like you, but she said she'd thought about it, and she didn't want to because that was standing still and she didn't want to waste her life, she said. Then she tore up the photograph of you and said that was her past, and the bear, too. So when she'd said good-bye and gone, I went upstairs and got them."

"She said good-bye to you?"

"Yes. She said she didn't want to see us go—you and me."

Silence. Wouldn't he talk? Couldn't he talk? *Fight it, Tory. Fight it.*

"I don't think that's a good reason for marrying anybody," she said, addressing the table, "but she had to choose between going on thinking about someone who didn't think about her, or marrying somebody who wanted her and going on with life."

She stopped. She wanted to cry out, to howl as Leo had howled that night—a long wail of loneliness and loss. But there was nothing to be sorry about—was there? Her father had said that he was going to stop travelling around; he was going to buy the Quinta do Rio and then slowly, so's not to hurt the aunts, they'd leave the Casa Fenix. The two of them. She would remember Philippa, he would remember Macau and her mother, and he couldn't help it if he hadn't been able to forget her. He hadn't had her very long; perhaps he had wanted to keep her memory with him so that he could feel she was still with him, going through life with him. It wasn't his fault, was it, if he loved her more than he loved Philippa?

And then she saw his hand.

He had picked up the little koala bear and his fingers had closed, tightened round it. He pressed convulsively, his knuckles showing white. She saw the little bear's head twist slowly round until the brown-button eyes and the flat black nose had gone, and only the back of the head showed. Tighter and tighter. The head was off.

She flashed an upward glance at her father. His face was ashen.

She saw his hand open; the little decapitated bear rolled onto the table and lay there in the long, long silence. Then Edmund spoke, and she realized that he was no longer beside her. He was at the door.

"Wait for me," he said. "I'll be back soon."

She turned, and their eyes met.

"With her," he added, and was gone.

She heard the front door close. Raising her eyes, she saw him going down the path to his car, putting on his coat as he went.

She sat still. The change from despair to hope, from hope to certainty, came gradually. Her mind followed her father along the wet streets as he drove nearer and nearer to the china shop. Round the corner into the shopping street, through the square, turn left, stop if the traffic lights were red, then on and on, and Philippa would be in there, waiting for . . .

For Lord Tancred. It was Lord Tancred, and not Edmund Brooke, she would be expecting to see. And Lord Tancred was coming here, and she, Tory, would have to tell him where Philippa was . . .

She heard his car stop at the gate. She saw his tall form, and heard the doorbell. She drew a deep breath and went to let him in. For one moment, no more, his fate hung in the balance. She had a message for him; she could deliver it at once; there was no need for him to enter the house.

But he had not waited for an invitation to enter. He gave her a nod and walked past her into the sitting room. She closed the front door and followed him. He spoke curtly.

"Tell Philippa I'm here, will you?"

"She isn't here."

"I don't understand. I told her I was coming here for her."

"Yes. But she had to go to the shop."

"What time did she go?"

"I'm not sure. I think about half an hour ago."

He said nothing. There was an angry frown on his face.

"Have you said good-bye to her?" he asked.

"Yes. She told me about Mr. Darlan."

"And what did you feel when you heard the news? Sorry? Glad?"

"I was sorry."

"Sorry the police didn't get him?"

"Sorry he got run over. If he hadn't run away, he wouldn't have been run over."

"Perhaps not." His tone was cold. "But in my view, he was doomed from the moment he left the train at Bayonne. I wonder if it occurs to you that if he hadn't offered himself as escort, he would probably be alive now?"

She made no answer. Something told her that his curt manner, his undisguised hostility rose from his growing uneasiness. He had expected Philippa to be waiting for him, and she had gone out. It could not have been the reception he had anticipated.

"You were lucky to get out of that adventure as well as you did," she heard him say. "Darlan was worse than a thief, but as Philippa thinks you should be spared the knowledge of how much worse, by all means let us spare you. Did she tell you she was going to marry me?"

"Yes."

"I won't ask you this time if you're glad or sorry, because I know the answer. All the same, I await your congratulations."

She made no reply. She turned to the table, picked up the photograph and completed the task of repairing it. He took a step forward and stood looking down at it.

"Why did you tear that up?" he asked.

"I didn't tear it up. Philippa did."

"It's yours, isn't it?"

"No. Hers."

"You gave it to her, I presume? I don't blame you for trying to advance your cause."

"I didn't give it to her. She had it already. It was on her dressing table—that and the koala bear. She always kept them there. My father won the bear on the day they got engaged, before he met my mother."

"She tore up the photograph?"

"Yes. She tore it up and threw it into the wastepaper basket, and I took it out and stuck it together because she'll be sorry, and she'll want it back."

"She won't be sorry, and she won't want it back."

"She might. She was crying a lot."

There was a pause.

"Will you please turn round and face me?" came his order.

She turned. There was no doubt now of his feelings towards her; his voice and his eyes both expressed them clearly.

"I have always considered you a liar," he said evenly. "Not a direct liar; a liar by implication. You are a very clever little girl, but you must not try to match your wits against those of an intelligent adult. You are trying to patch up, to stick together, something which has come apart. You're wasting your time. I advise you to give up. When your father comes to fetch you, I would advise you to tell him that you have given up. He—"

"He came already." She corrected the un-English phrasing. "He came."

"He came here?"

"Yes."

"Then why are you not on your way to school?"

"Because he didn't stay. He went away again."

"Where did he go?"

"He went to the shop."

"Which shop?"

"The china shop, where Philippa went."

His face paled.

"Are you telling the truth?"

"Yes. I don't tell lies. My father came, and I was mending the photograph and I told him that Philippa had torn it up and she was crying, and he crushed the koala bear in his hand and its head came off and he asked me where Philippa had gone, and I told him, and he went there, too. And if he doesn't come back soon, I'll be late starting for school."

"He couldn't have gone to the shop. Philippa told me that she said good-bye to him yesterday."

Her eyes lifted and met his fully and then fell again.

"They aren't saying good-bye," she said.

She was unable to assess, then or throughout her life, how long the silence lasted. She was under no illusion as to how he was feeling. She knew that he was suffering torments because he was facing a future—as she had faced a future—in which Philippa belonged to someone else. If he felt anything like she had felt all this morning, he was to be pitied and she ought to feel sorry for him, and in a way she did, but all she could really think of were two people who meant more to her than anybody else in the world. All she could see was a future in which her father had ceased to live with a memory.

She heard Lord Tancred's voice, and with difficulty brought her mind back to the room. She glanced up at him; his face was expressionless.

"There was a time," he told her quietly, "when I regretted not having children. Since knowing you, I have ceased to want them."

She waited until the front door had crashed behind him; then she picked up the koala bear. There would be no time to mend it here; she would take it to school and sew on its head.

School. She thought with sudden pleasure of the smell of new textbooks, the challenge of new, empty exercise books. The Paget twins had said that she would find herself behind the rest of the class because the teaching at the convent hadn't been up to English standards. Well, there might be some catching up to do. But she wouldn't be behind for long.